Sabine Baring-Gould

The Gaverocks

A Tale of the Cornish Coast - Vol. I

Sabine Baring-Gould

The Gaverocks
A Tale of the Cornish Coast - Vol. I

ISBN/EAN: 9783337082574

Printed in Europe, USA, Canada, Australia, Japan

Cover: Foto ©Andreas Hilbeck / pixelio.de

More available books at **www.hansebooks.com**

THE GAVEROCKS

A TALE OF THE CORNISH COAST

BY THE

AUTHOR OF 'JOHN HERRING' 'MEHALAH' &c.

IN THREE VOLUMES

VOL. I.

LONDON

SMITH, ELDER, & CO., 15 WATERLOO PLACE

1887

CONTENTS

OF

THE FIRST VOLUME

THE GAVEROCKS.

CHAPTER I.

THE BROTHERS.

THE road was bad. To speak with accuracy, the road was not a road, but a track. To be more accurate still, it was not a track, but a series of tracks cut by cart and carriage and gig wheels in the turf, and through it to the sparry stone beneath, that worked up in lumps like sugar, but which were so hard that the wheel of a laden wain would not crush them.

Along this course—this tangled skein of wheel tracks, over a moor, bounced and pitched and lurched and dived a tax-cart with two men in it, one very much older than the other, for in fact he was the father.

The father drove, whilst the son sat holding to the back of the seat with one hand, to the side with the other, and with his eyes fixed on the horse's ears. The driver was more accustomed to the motions of the cart, was able to balance himself without holding a rail.

Hardly a tree was visible. The down was covered with short grass, dotted over with dark-green clumps of gorse, spotted with gold where stray flowers bloomed, but covered with bursting seed-pods. Here and there a hedge appeared with thorns on the top, curling over away from the west, and leafing only on the nether surface.

Beyond, where the sun was setting in a bed of quivering fire, lay the Atlantic, with the horizon half-way up the sky.

The horse or the driver, or the horse and driver together, groped among the ruts for the least profound and the least knobby at bottom —groped with the wheels of the tax-cart ; did not like one rut, tried another, then a third, after that went recklessly at any rut that offered, found that did not succeed, once more went through the course of selection, and finally abandoned the exercise of intelligence and reason for happy-go-lucky, like many a man at the outstart of life who tries one line, then another, and finally allows himself to jolt on in whatever

rut receives him.   In vain did horse, or driver,
or horse and driver together, endeavour to find
ruts to the gauge of the cart; all the convey-
ances that had ever gone before and cut for
themselves grooves had been just too broad or
just too narrow, so that the tax-cart always
went with one wheel deep in a furrow and the
other high on the turf.

Between the driver and the setting sun and
sea, fused into one sheet of flame, stood a house
—a long, low house, all roof, except on the
side that was approached by the cart, the side
that looked inland.   As the road was not a
road, but a skein of tracks, so the side was not
a side, but an irregular face.   It was formed
of a front with doorway and low, wide windows
and two uneven projecting gables, one at each
extremity.   About this house clustered some
miserable trees—beech, that had died at their
heads, and lived a sickly, apologetic life in the
lower branches, where a few shrivelled leaves
appeared.   The trunks of these trees were
inclined inland, at an angle so acute that anyone unaccustomed to the habits of trees on the
coast would have expected them to fall at the
first puff of wind.

This house was Towan. It belonged, at the beginning of the century which we honour with living in it, to Hender Gaverock (the name pronounced Gav'r-ock), a man of some property—in fact, a small country squire.

Towan was situated in the parish of St. Kevin, on the north coast of Cornwall, about four miles from Padstow and twelve from Wadebridge.

The cart in which the two men rode belonged to Hender Gaverock, and contained him and his younger son Constantine, a fine young man with hair auburn—a warm chestnut, and with blue eyes. There was a certain resemblance between the two men, but also a striking dissimilarity. The same features and colour of hair, but the young man was smooth and refined, and the old one was rugged and uncouth. There was in the father a hardness, a headstrong look in the eyes, a selfwill in the modelling of the lips, a domineer in the cut of the nose. As for the son, Constantine, his mouth expressed much weakness. It lacked brightness and was overcast with discontent. His skin was clearer than that of his father; it was,

plain at a glance that it had not been exposed
of late to the elements.

'There, boy, is mother standing in the doorway expecting us!' exclaimed old Hender, who
was driving, and he pointed before him with
his whip.

'*Us!*' repeated Constantine; '*me*, you
mean, father; I have been absent for a twelvemonth in Nankivel's fusty office—I hate it.'

'Oh, Con! you will become a great lawyer
in time.'

Constantine shrugged his shoulders and
made no answer to this remark. Presently,
after a moment of brooding, he said :

'It is a hard thing that I should be moped
up in a lawyer's office, whilst Gerans, because
he is the eldest son, should be obliged to do
nothing. Why is he not now at the door with
my mother, looking out for me?'

'Because, you fool, he is out hunting.'

'He can go hunting, boating, shooting, but
I must use the pen and have no horse, or boat,
or gun. I am nothing, and he is everything.
He is the first-born and the heir, born with
a silver spoon in his mouth. He has all the
love and ambition of the house fixed on him,

and poor I am driven into a far country to eat husks with the swine—I mean into a dirty sty of a lawyer's office.'

' You will see, Con, the fatted calf will be killed for you.'

' Oh, I want no extraordinary festivity made in honour of my return, as if I were a prodigal son. I am not that, but most respectable, steady, dusty, and dry. A lawyer's clerk must be all that. It is part of the business.'

'No, Con, you are no prodigal son, and Gerans is not like the elder brother in the parable. He doesn't grumble and begrudge you anything; no one is more delighted than he at your return. You are the younger, and must accept the position.'

The old man was red in the face and sulky. He was irritated at the mood of his son, who returned after a long absence grumbling and discontented because he had not the place and advantages of his elder brother.

' There'll be something for you after all, Con,' said the squire. ' But wait and see what it is. You will in the end settle near Towan. I reckon it is a place you would like to spend your days near.'

'I don't know,' observed the young man with a shrug; 'I like civilisation. You wouldn't, I reckon, like to be taken by the scruff of the neck and pitched out of this century into the barbarism of a hundred years ago. I feel like that, when returning from a town, with its polish and enlightenment and good roads, to this wild moor—rough, gloomy, roadless.'

The trap drew up in front of the house, and Hender Gaverock slowly dismounted. He was a strange old man. He wore high boots and a waterman's jersey under a rough, long-tailed coat, weather-beaten and discoloured. On ordinary occasions he wore no cap or hat, but a surprising head of reddish-grey hair, harsh and coarse, that blew about in the wind and looked more like a mass of frowsy heather. He never wore a hat except on Sundays and when he went into a town, or to pay a call; then he covered his head with a shaggy white beaver, almost as rough and tangled as his natural head of hair. This day, as he had been to Padstow, he did wear his hat, at the back of his head. 'Hats blow off and blow away,' said old Gaverock, 'but it would take such a

gale as would uproot our Cornish cliffs to carry
the natural cover off my crown.'

A crimson kerchief was knotted round his
neck, the ends depended over his breast. In
very stormy and wet weather the utmost protection he allowed himself was to take this kerchief from his neck, tie it over his head, and
knot it under his chin.

In front of the windows and main door of
the house ran a slated walk the full length of
the face. Here Hender Gaverock was wont
to pace with great strides in his water-boots.
The slate slabs at each extremity of the walk
were marked with concentric circles. For,
when standing there, Hender turned on his
heels when he reached the last slate, and scored
the rings when he revolved on his iron-shod
heels.

As the Squire dismounted he shouted for a
groom, but none appeared. Then he shouted
again, and swore.

'By Golly!' he said, 'where are the men?
What has become of them. I want my horse
to be taken.'

He addressed his wife, who stood in the
porch, a delicate-faced, sweet, faded lady, wear-

ing a white frilled cap. Although the words were spoken to her, Gaverock did not turn his face towards her, but roared his words into the wide space before the door, leaving the echoes to repeat them in her ear.

'Golly! he does look curious, I protest,' exclaimed Hender, standing with his legs apart, and his hands in his pockets, looking at Con as he dismounted.

Then Mrs. Gaverock came down the steps of the porch, ran forward, put out both her hands to clasp Constantine as he leaped to the ground, her timid face fluttering with smiles and suffused with tears—tears and smiles, the common progeny of joy.

'Out of the way, wife!' shouted Hender; 'don't molly-coddle the boy. Stand back, Con; let your mother look at you. Lord! what sort of a coat do you call that?' The father caught his younger son by the shoulder, twirled him about roughly, forward, backward, from side to side, and laughed. 'Town fashions, eh? my word as a gentleman! What jackanapes you young men make of yourselves, and think to set up as bucks and dandies. Where is Mathews? I want the horse and trap to be taken.'

'I believe, husband,' said the old lady, 'the hounds and hunters are in Nantsillan Grove, and all the men have run after them and the fox. You were not expected so soon.'

'Very well,' said the squire, 'Con and I can take the trap round and unharness. Come, sir, buck and dandy though you think yourself, jackanapes though you seem in my eyes, let me see that you are true Cornish Gaverock to the core still. Off with your coat, Constantine!'

'What do you want me to do, father?'

'The men have run after the hounds, of course. I don't blame them. Let me see that you are not a town fop. Come round to the yard and unharness and rub the mare's ears.'

'I am not an ostler,' answered Constantine, sulkily. He folded his arms over his breast and looked down, his brows knitted, his lips puffed out.

'Well,' exclaimed old Hender, 'here's a twelvemonth you've been away, sitting on a stool like a broody hen, hatching nothing but legal mischief. Has that taken the manhood out of you? If so, I'll none of you. I'll disown a milksop. Take this trap round and

unharness. What! have you forgotten how to
unrig a horse?'

'Hender, the boy is tired,' pleaded Mrs.
Gaverock.

'Tired? What with? Sitting is natural
with him, and he has been but sitting outside
a coach a few hours, and a little longer in the
gig. Old woman, do not interfere. What I
choose I will have. What I order must be
done. What I set my head on must be carried
out. Come, take the mare out and groom her.'

The tone of command his father assumed
angered Constantine. The hectoring, domineering ways of the old man had been endured when
he was a boy, but he was a man now, and he
was determined to resist.

'I will not,' answered Constantine, surlily.

The old man looked at his son angrily. His
face was effervescing with life.

'Lord!' he exclaimed, 'you've not unlearnt
country ways in Exeter, I hope. You were
always a bit of a milksop and your mother's
darling. I bore with it when you were a boy,
but thought it unnatural. It is twice as unnatural in a man. You should wear petticoats
and a bonnet. But—what have we got on?'

He took Constantine by the shoulders once more, and again spun him round.

'Mercy on us! what a dandy we are!—a green coat with brass buttons, like a buttercup meadow! a pair of waistcoats, one figured satin underneath and the other above it of nankin!' He stood back, placed his hands on his hips and roared with laughter. 'Come, you damned dandified fool!' he shouted, 'off with the coat at once, I order, and unharness and groom the mare.'

Constantine did not stir. His dogged look intensified. All at once, his father went to him, tripped up his heels, and cast him sprawling on his back.

Then Hender burst out laughing, and as his wife started forward to the aid of her prostrate son he restrained her with his arm, and said, 'A sulky ill-conditioned hound! torn his city coat, has he! so much the better. The rent will serve to let the wild wind in to blow his sour humours away.' Then, without another word he went towards the stable-yard, leading the horse and cart, to do himself what his town-spoiled son refused to soil his hands with doing.

'Never heed this, Con,' said his mother.

'You know what a delight father takes in showing his masterhood. You must put up with his ways—they mean kindness, though roughly expressed. To any one who knows him, it is an outbreak of affection, quite as much as my kisses.'

'I wish I had not returned to Towan,' answered Constantine, rising with the help of his mother's hand. 'I cannot, I will not, endure this treatment.'

'My dear, dear Con!' said his mother, 'you have come home to gladden my heart with the sight of you. There, forget the cast. You must not take it amiss. It is the way in which your father shows his paternal love and delight at seeing you home.'

'I have been away for a twelvemonth, and this is my first salutation when I come home. He will kick me downstairs next, and you will affirm it is to do me honour; pitch me out of the window, and be comforted to know it is evidence of his predilection. I do not like these ebullitions of fatherly love—they may do among Choctaws and Otaheite Indians; or even——'

'Hush! hush! Con! Remember that he

is your father; you must not judge his conduct and disparage his manners.' She put her hand over his lips as he muttered something about 'Ourang-outangs and kangaroos.'

Constantine kissed the hand, then his mother clasped him to her heart and burst into tears.

At that moment the clatter of horses' hoofs and the ring of many voices were echoed by the grey walls. Old Squire Gaverock ran out from the stable-yard, and called, 'Back, Rose! Got the brush, eh?'

'No, Guardy! no brush when cub-hunting,' came the answer to the question.

A party of returning huntsmen swept up; with them, on a white horse, a graceful girl in hat and riding habit.

'Come in! come in all of you! Hunters always, proverbially, are hungry. Had a good run? Scent lie well? No necks, no knees broken? Necks of men and knees of horses?'

'Gerans, take my rein,' said the girl, calling to the elder son, who rode behind her, and casting the reins towards him as she leaped from her horse. Gerans had caught sight of his brother, and ran to him with

sparkling eyes and extended hand, and so
neglected to attend to Rose.   When he turned
to assist her to dismount, she was on her feet
already.

'Late—sluggish and sleepy as usual, Cousin
Gerans!' she said; 'and now, mind that
Phœbus be well cared for—he is very hot and
tired.   Where is my cousin Constantine?   I
want an introduction, and hope to find him
more on the alert than you.'

She looked about her.   'What! that
gentleman in tatters!

> Hush! hark, the dogs do bark,
> The beggars are coming to Towan,
> Some in rags, and some in jags——'

Constantine coloured at the reference to his
torn coat.   'I apologise for appearing before
you in this figure,' he said; but she interrupted
him with—'Why! bless me, Gerans! Are you
twins?   You are so much alike that you must
mistake each other for self at times.'

Strangely alike the brothers were—the same
hair, the same features, the same build, the
same tricks of movement; only in expression
were they unlike—Gerans frank and good-
humoured, Constantine moody and dissatisfied.

Rose did not wait for an answer to her question. Her quick blue eye had caught sight of a young man turning his horse to ride away. 'Here!' she exclaimed, catching up her habit with one hand, and waving the whip imperiously with the other, 'no skulking off, Mr. Penhalligan. I have just caught you in the act of executing a retreat, when the general sounded a summons to table. Stay!'

'Miss Trewhella, one must be driven from your presence—one is not disposed to skulk from it,' answered the young man, a dark handsome man, seated on a rough cob.

'Well said, Mr. Penhalligan,' laughed the girl. 'There is a polish of politeness about you which is so rare an element at Towan that we prize it when it is found. I doubt not but that in proper hands something may be made out of you.'

'Anything may be made out of me, if you, Miss Trewhella, will put your hand to the moulding.'

'I have neither the patience nor the skill,' said Rose Trewhella, laughing; 'I am doing my best to civilise Uncle Hender, but the result does not reward the pains.' Then, suddenly, in an altered tone, 'Why is not your sister Loveday out with us to-day?'

'Because I have no second horse on which she can ride.'

'Oh, you bad brother—like all men, selfish. You should have stayed at home, and sent her out.'

'Then, consider, there was no groom to look after her.'

'I have none to-day but my cousin, Gerans. If it were possible for me to ride without a groom, surely it was possible also for Loveday.'

'Every gentleman in the field, Miss Trewhella, is your dutiful servant.'

'And the same to Loveday. Have you noticed how I have pouted all day? It has been because your sister was not with us.'

'How do you do, Dennis?' said Gerans, coming up beside the dark young man, and patting the neck of his cob. 'What sort of a run have you had? How did this mare keep up?'

Penhalligan shook his head. 'Only a cob I can't keep hunters.'

'How is your sister?' asked Gerans, passing over the reply without notice. 'Look!

here is Constantine. Do you see him? He has returned home for a change.'

Constantine came up, awkwardly, with his eyes on the ground; but that may have been due to disgust at appearing in a torn coat. He held out his hand.

Dennis Penhalligan did not meet the extended fingers; he pretended to overlook the proffered hand. 'Constantine and I must have a talk,' he said; then he turned the head of his horse and rode away to the stable-yard to hitch up his beast.

CHAPTER II.

ROSE TREWHELLA.

THE party of huntsmen were assembled in the hall of Towan House. The hall was low, lighted by a long five-light granite window looking to the east. It had an immense open granite fireplace, in which a log was smouldering upon a pair of andirons, banked up with peat, that diffused an agreeable odour through the room. The hall was panelled with oak and ornamented with stags' horns. Towan in past times was said to have had a deer-park, but the park had consisted merely of a walled paddock of some ten acres, in which was a spring of pure water, with some gnarled, crouching thorns above it.

The wall of the deer paddock remained in places, but the greater portion was broken down; of the deer, all that remained were the few horns on the wall, poor and stunted as the trees that grew on that coast. The horns were fitted into very rudely cut heads of oak, shaped by a village carpenter in past times.

The Gaverocks were an old Cornish family, untainted by intermixture with Saxon or Norman blood. They had married and intermarried with ancient families of extraction as pure, and of name as Keltic, as their own : the Killiowes, the Bodrugans, the Mennynnicks, the Nanspians, the Rosvargus, and the Chynoweths. It cannot be said that they had fallen from their high estate, for they had lost none of their land, but they had remained stationary, whilst other families had mounted and others had declined. Two hundred—nay, even a hundred—years ago there was scarcely a parish in the West of England without two, three, or more resident gentry in it, owning good estates, dividing the parish between them, marrying in and out with each other, and leaving yeomen to flourish in the interstices between their estates. Most have disappeared. Here and there one remains, who has bought up his failing neighbours, and established himself as sole squire in the place. Among these petty gentry the lord of the manor exercised pre-eminence.   He had certain rights over the lands of his neighbours, which they were unable to resist, and he unwilling to resign.   Sometimes there were two manors in the same parish, and then he whose manor included the church-town was accorded the pre-eminence.   A silent and mysterious revolution has taken place in the social conditions.   The small gentry and most of the yeomanry have disappeared—how is not so easy to establish as the fact of their disappearance.[1]

The old country gentlemen of small estate, but of splendid pedigree, farmed their own lands, and were not ashamed to have their mansions surrounded by stacks and barns.[2] Indeed, in many instances the grand entrance

[1] The parish of Bratton Clovelly, in Devon, covers an area of little over 8,000 acres.   Down to 1750 there were eight gentle families resident in it: landowners, with right to bear arms. The Willoughbies, an elder branch of the family of Lord Willoughby d'Eresby, the Coryndons, Langesfords, Calmadys, Burnebys, the Parkers, ancestors of Lord Morley, the Incledons, and the Luxmores, all have vanished from it.

[2] The old house of the Parkers in Bratton Clovelly, Ellacott, inherited from the heiress of Ellacott, but of more recent date than the marriage, has the house forming one side, and 'cob' barns, and stables, and cowsheds enclosing a quadrangle and opening into it.   All the dwelling-house windows looked into this farmyard.   A pair of handsome gates—now destroyed— admitted to farmyard and dwelling-house alike.

was through the farmyard by a paved way, between heaps and pits of dung, to the manor-house, which formed one side, whilst outhouses, stables, and barns enclosed the quadrangle.

Devon and Cornwall are strewn with these old mansions, like empty snail-shells. The gentry have left them, died or disappeared, and they are converted into farmhouses or cottages. The advance of civilisation had so far affected the Gaverocks that they had swept away their quadrangle and rebuilt their farm outhouses behind instead of in front of the house. Turf now grew where the stable-yard had been for centuries, and a few eschalonia grew before the windows, defied the winds and flowered like alpine roses. But if the face of the house had gained in respectability by the removal of the yard, it had lost in shelter. The east wind now rushed unbroken against it, and drove in at the porch, slamming doors through-out the house whenever any one entered or quitted the mansion by the main entrance. The characteristic feature of all these old dwell-ing-houses had been that they never looked out upon the world; they were screened be-hind walls, and every window blinked into a court or an enclosed garden. The courts were sometimes many—cells into which the sun entered and where it was caught as in a trap, but out of which the rude winds were excluded. Now that this feature of Towan was effaced, Towan was a draughty place — battered by storm, piped through, screamed into, swashed about by wind and rain.

Miss Rose Trewhella, who called Squire Gaverock her uncle and his sons her cousins, was no relation by blood, though a connexion by marriage. Her father had married a lady who was somehow related to some lady who had at some time married a Gaverock. Her father was dead, and had left his daughter to the care of his friend of many years—Hender Gaverock, of Towan. Trewhella (his Christian name was Roseclear) had lived in another part of the country, but he had visited his friend annually for a month at Towan, and Gaverock had annually returned the visit for the same length of time. Till the death of Mr. Trewhella, the young Gaverocks had seen nothing of Rose. He had not brought her with him when he came to Towan, because Hender had no daughter with whom she might associate when there.

Rose was Roseclear Trewhella's only child. She was a wayward, spoiled girl; was very pretty, and conscious both of her beauty and of the fact that she was an heiress. She was delicately fair, with hair like gold, and eyes blue as the summer sea, and a complexion so clear and bright that no one could look on her and deny that she had been given at her baptism the most appropriate name that could have been selected to describe her.

On coming to Towan, Rose had settled herself into her new quarters with perfect aptitude, had won her way to the heart of Mrs. Gaverock, whom, however, she bewildered, exercised a sort of daring authority over the Squire, which he endured because it was not worth his trouble to resist, and treated Gerans as her groom and errand-boy. She was good-natured and lively as long as she had her own way; when—which was rarely—she was crossed, she pouted, and managed to make every one about her uncomfortable. She was not in the smallest degree shy. Brought up in the society of men, who flattered and made much of her, she preferred their company to that of women. But though she liked to be with men, and be made much of by men, she was dimly conscious of an inarticulate, undefined craving for the companionship of a woman to whom she could empty her mind, of whom she could exact nothing but sympathy. Her mother had died too early for her to be even a reminiscence. On arriving at Towan she had made the acquaintance of Loveday Penhalligan, and had been drawn to her as she had been attracted by no other woman.

Loveday was an orphan, like herself; pretty, but of quite another order of beauty, with olive skin, dark hair, and large soft umber eyes. Loveday lived with her brother Dennis in a cottage, called Nantsillan, rented of the Squire.

Dennis Penhalligan was a surgeon, a young man, who had come to the place about five years before, having bought the practice. Dennis was a poor man; his capital had not permitted of his purchasing any other than a very humble practice. He had spent his little fortune on his own education and on thus establishing himself. The neighbourhood was a three-sided one—one side being the sea—and was but sparsely inhabited.

Dennis Penhalligan was a tall, well-built

man, with black hair, an olive complexion, and
dark keen eyes. His poverty, the hardships he
had undergone in elbowing his way in life, had
taken the joy and elasticity from his spirits, and
had given a bitterness to his mood unusual to
one of his age. He was the intellectual superior of all his neighbours, and he held himself
aloof from association with them, in cold and
sour contempt of their narrowness of interests
and pettiness of aim. His patients complained
of callousness in his treatment of their sufferings.
He did not administer to them that sympathy
which they desired equally with medicine. A
surgeon who has walked the hospitals looks on
his patients as cases, not persons. But when
he begins to practise for a fee, he finds that
persons insist on being considered persons and
not cases. They demand of their medical
attendant that he shall have, or simulate (it
matters nothing which), an individual interest in
them. Every practitioner should place himself
in the hands of an actor to qualify him for success in his professional career.

Dennis was too haughtily truthful, too scornful of weakness, to pretend to what he did not
possess. When called to the side of a hypochon-

driac, he treated the case both lightly and con-
temptuously. When he saw that the complaint
was trifling, he did not make a second and a third
call, and this was resented. People are often
ready to pay to be esteemed sick.

The result was that Penhalligan was un-
popular. The people of the neighbourhood
preferred sending ten miles to fetch an inferior
practitioner, who ministered to their humours
rather than physicked their disease, rather than
summon Dennis, who was at their door.

Dennis chafed at the non-recognition of his
merits. He despised the old, ignorant, drunken
doctor who stole his patients from under his
nose, but he was too proud and too conscientious
to alter his conduct.

From the hour of his first interview with
Rose Trewhella, the fair, cheerful girl had exercised an extraordinary fascination over Dennis.
Her openness contrasted with his reserve, her
cheerfulness with his gravity, no less than her
clear complexion and golden locks contrasted
with his sallow face and black hair.

She was fully aware of the admiration she
had aroused in the heart of the village doctor,
and she was perfectly content to coquet with

him, to repulse him, as the caprice prompted
and his devotion amused or wearied her. He
had made no deeper impression on her heart
or fancy than any other man among the many
that fluttered around her. If he was regardless of his patients' feelings, so also was she ;
in this one point alone were they alike.

The table in the hall was spread. Joints,
pies, tarts, cream, cakes, fruit, tea for those who
liked, and, for those who preferred, cider and
wine. A merry party was assembled about it,
of whom not the least merry was Rose, who
had changed her habit for a pretty evening dress.
Only Constantine was troubled and silent. He
could not forget his fall. He had changed his
coat, but not his humour. Dennis affected
cheerfulness. When in the society of Rose he
was happy as far as his morose nature was
capable of being galvanised into happiness.

A good many young men and half a
dozen ladies were present, laughing, joking
each other about the events of the day's ride,
or about accidents and mistakes on past occasions.

Presently some one started the subject of
the seashore and the phosphorescence of the

waves, which had been unusually beautiful the night previous.

'Let us go to the beach,' said one, 'and see whether the waves are on fire this evening.'

The proposal was agreed to by acclamation. The meal was rapidly concluded, and the merry, eager throng of young people swept out of the hall and away, laughing, talking, down a path to Nantsillan Cove.

Rose remained. She was somewhat tired with the day's ride, and did not care for a scramble down the cliffs. She stood in the window, with her hands behind her back, looking after the party, till the last had passed round the wing of the house and had disappeared. Then she turned, and started to see Dennis Penhalligan still in the room.

'Why are you not gone with the rest?' she asked.

'I had no inclination to go. May I not remain in the sun if I am cold?'

'Of course. But I do not understand you; the sun has set.'

'I was speaking metaphorically.'

She pursed up her lips. 'If you remain to enjoy my society, you remain for woeful disappointment. The only good things I had to say are all said; my wit is wholly flown. My conversation is like a pottle of market-woman's strawberries, where the good fruit is at the top and underneath is utter squash. I have but a few notes of the nightingale, and all the rest are twitters.' She took her straw hat and swung it by the strings. 'It must be very pleasant on the beach,' she said after a while.

'I can well believe it.'

'Then why do you not go thither?'

'How can you ask the question when you remain?'

'I prefer to be here.'

'So do I.'

'Why so?' She turned towards him and thrust forth her pretty pouting red lips.

'Because the queen of the swarm is here.'

'I remain because I want to be alone.'

'That is your reason, is it, Miss Rose?'

'Yes; but I am not alone.'

'Very well,' said Dennis, colouring. 'I will leave you directly. It is not necessary to be so frank with me. Will you not sit down?—only for a moment, and then I will go.'

'I can stand.'

'Yes; but I want you to listen calmly to me.'

'I cannot be calm. It is no more in my nature than it is in that of the restless Atlantic.'

'I pray you, if you cannot be calm, be patient with me,' said Dennis. 'I want to say two words to you. They are soon said. I entreat you, be quiet and listen to me. Will you, Miss Rose, or will you not?' He stepped up to her and stood before her.

'Very well,' she said, with a sigh and a shrug of her pretty little shoulders. 'But pray be quick; I am tired.'

'Miss Rose, you have behaved strangely to me. At times you have drawn me towards you, as though you liked my company; at others you have scarcely noticed my presence. To-day, although I was constantly at your side, you barely deigned to observe me, to cast at me a look or a word, till, hurt and sore, I was about to leave, when suddenly you turned on me all smiles, called me to your side, forbade my escape, and during supper singled me out for your sallies. Have I offended you? If so, tell me how. Have I obtained your pardon? If so, tell me by what means. Your behaviour towards me passes my comprehension; you are a swaying magnet, presenting alternatively the positive and the negative poles.'

'Positive and negative poles! Mr. Penhalligan,' said Rose, swinging her hat vigorously and keeping him at a distance with it. 'You asked for two words, and after a long preface you have produced them. Positive and negative poles! I protest; these words are vastly beyond my poor comprehension.'

'What has made you angry with me?'

'Angry! I am not angry. It takes something to make me angry.'

'Am not I something?'

'Oh, nothing, nothing.'

'Miss Rose, do not be cruel; you torture me.'

'I torture no one. Certain people are like the Indian fakirs, they skewer themselves. There,' she said, putting forth her hand, 'strike palms; we are hunting comrades. Tally-ho!'

'Comrades only? Comrades in the field—nothing more?

'Certainly not. What more could you wish?'

'I could wish a great deal more. I do wish for more!'

'Have you ever caught the phosphorescent flash in the sea?'

'Never.'

'Have you ever wished to do so?'

'Never.'

'Then do not desire to catch what eludes being caught. Here come the maids to clear away tea. Good-night, Mr. Penhalligan. You had better go to the beach and see the waves break into lightning.'

'Is this all you have to say to me?'

'All.'

He turned away, took up his hat, and went to the porch. When he reached the door he halted, looked into his hat, and then turned his head inquiringly towards Rose. She met his eyes, smiled, and screwed up her lips, and whirled her hat round, making with it complete revolutions in the air. Then he set his cap on his head and drew the door after him. Rose stood considering for a moment, with her slender finger to her lips; then a pretty dimple came in her cheeks, and she laughed, put on her straw hat, and went out ; looked after the surgeon, and seeing that he was on his way home, and had not taken the path to the Cove, she threw a kerchief round her shoulders, and tripped lightly down the path to the sea.

CHAPTER III.

PORTH-IERNE.

Dennis Penhalligan walked from Towan with his head down. He was not disappointed with his rebuff, because he had not expected encouragement; because, moreover, he was accustomed to meet with discouragement in all he undertook and at every turn. Some men are never cast down, never have the heart taken out of them; such men are either endowed with extraordinary buoyancy or with extraordinary conceit. Dennis was not sanguine by nature, he was not conceited, but he was not diffident. He knew his own abilities, but he knew also that successes are for the fools and knaves. The fools are endowed by Providence with luck to counterbalance their folly, and the wise are burdened with conscience, which prevents them profiting by their wisdom.

The cottage inhabited by Dennis Penhalligan

and his sister was hardly five minutes' walk
from Towan. It lay in a coomb into which
flowed the rill from the spring in the old deer-
park. This rill did not form the glen, it was
merely an affluent of the Nantsillan brook
which traversed the coomb. Under the brow
of the hills grew some trees, their tops tortured
to death the moment they rose sufficiently high
to catch the wind, but forming shelter and
giving shadow beneath them. Bedded among
these stunted and sloping trees was the cottage.

Dennis opened the door and walked in.

'Please, sir,' said the servant-girl, a child
of fifteen, 'Miss Loveday be agone down to
the Cove. The gentlefolks comed after her
from Towan and tooked her off.'

Dennis nodded, stood in the door, considered, and after a slight hesitation moved
down the coomb to the sea.

The cottage was on the way to the beach
—that is, on one way. A shorter path from
Towan led down the face of the cliff, but it
was somewhat dangerous. Prudent counsels
had prevailed with the young people, and
instead of risking the steep descent they had

taken the round by Nantsillan, and in doing so had picked up Loveday.

Dennis was not in his best humour. He was vexed at his sister's departure. He knew that no harm would befall her, but he was unhappy himself, and he could ill brook that she was merry-making whilst he was troubled. In this he was selfish. But he had an excuse. He and his sister were alone together in the world, and she was the only person to whom he opened his heart, and from whom he could endure sympathy.

He descended the coomb towards the shore. The evening was rapidly closing in. A warm orange light hung over the Atlantic to the west, where the sun had set two hours ago. The sea itself was leaden grey. As he approached he heard the roar of the ever-restless ocean, and saw the breakers flashing over the reefs.

The slope declined rapidly. The glen was narrow, wooded in laps and folds, heather-clad where exposed. The stream worked its way through black peat lying under sand, in little falls, till it reached the edge of the sea-fretted cliff, where it danced over it in a small but pretty cascade that gave its name to the coomb.

Nant is the Cornish word for a waterfall. At this point the path left the turf, and descended a few feet over the broken edges of a shelf of slate-rock. At this point also Dennis caught up Rose Trewhella rapidly descending the cliff from Towan.

'What!' exclaimed the young surgeon. 'You have changed your mind?'

'Oh dear, yes. I change like the weather-cock.'

'In everything?'

'Certainly—in all things; it is not men only who are, as the poet says, "To one thing constant never." Where are the rest? I came to Nantsillan Cove supposing you would not be there.'

'They are yonder. I will help you down the steps to them.'

The steps consisted of the irregular natural projections of the slate rock, which here rose in strata almost perpendicular.

'Lend me your hand,' said Rose. 'Let us move more quickly. I want to be with the others. See! they are surely going into Porth-Ierne.'

Penhalligan led the lively girl carefully

down the descent, from one jagged step to another. She leaped from the last to the beach. The shore was not, however, a smooth sweep of sand in a crescent between the projecting heads of Cardue and Sillan Point. The sand was ribbed with sharp slate ridges running up from the water to the cliffs, resembling the dorsal fins of sharks that were buried under the sand. Where the strata were soft the stone had been dissolved by the waves, but between the clayey yellow beds were bands of blue slate that rang to a hammer like a bell and cut like razors. Dennis helped Rose over these ridges. Some were three feet, some a foot high, all were fretted like saws. Rose skipped lightly across them.

'Why have they gone into Porth-Ierne?' she asked, and pointed to a cavern in the black promontory of Cardue that formed the southern horn of the bay. The northern promontory was Sillan Point. 'Surely they are not going through it into Sandymouth, and so home?'

'No,' answered Penhalligan, 'they cannot do that. The tide is rising and rolling in at the Sandymouth opening of the tunnel. Our friends have entered because without there is too much light for them to observe the phosphorescence of the water, or at all events to see it to perfection. Within that natural gateway night dwells, and there they can stand and see the liquid fire swirl past their feet.'

'Do you often have the sea on fire here?'

'No—occasionally, when the water is warm, and there have been south-westerly winds. Sometimes before a great storm.'

'Is the sea phosphorescent this evening?'

'I suspect so. Observe your feet on the sand.'

Rose looked down. She was treading on sand that had been just overwashed by a wave. As she trod, a flash of pale white light surrounded her little foot, a flash as faint as distant summer lightning.

'How strange!' said Rose. 'The touch of my foot seems to kindle a flame.'

'Not the touch of your foot only,' said Dennis.

Rose tossed her head and withdrew her hand from his.

'See! when I remove my foot the fire

ceases.   I protest, the flame is very transient, and very innocuous.'

Nantsillan Cove was a horseshoe bay gnawed by the Atlantic surge out of the rocky coast, which rose from two hundred to three hundred feet above the sand and sea.   The southern horn of the bay, Cardue Head, was pierced at the neck by a tunnel worked through by the waves on both sides acting on a loop in the contorted strata.   This archway was some twenty feet high.   In time, perhaps, it would become larger, and the roof fall in, and finally Cardue Head would become an island.   This tunnel was called Porth-Ierne, or the Iron Gate At low tide, with some picking of way among pools, and scrambling over boulders, it was possible to pass completely through from Nant-sillan Cove into Sandymouth Bay.   Even when the tide was flowing, when the sea was calm, it could be entered on a shelf of slate rock that ran in half the way, forming a ledge on the side, from which the water might be watched as it raced in from the farther side, where the tide flowed earlier than in the Cove.   The waves that swept into the bay were reflexed by Sillan Point, whereas those at the western entrance bowled in from the open ocean. The party of young people was entering the tunnel as Rose and the doctor reached the sands. Their merry voices rang cheerily from the black rocks above the murmur of the rhythmic waves.

'Loveday is there!' exclaimed Rose. 'I see her. My cousin Constantine is lifting her now on to the ledge.'

'Yes,' answered Dennis, 'Loveday is there. That is why I have come on to the Cove.'

'You did not calculate on finding *me* here?'

'There is no calculating on what is fickle.'

'You are not complimentary.'

'I attribute to you the quality you flatter yourself on possessing.'

'It is one thing to give oneself a bad character, another to have it given one by a second person. Loveday!' called Rose, and ran forward.

Dennis's sister was only a few yards in front; she was standing on the rocky ledge that stood draped with sea-tangles three feet above the sand. The vast black cavern was behind her. She was dressed in a simple white evening 'sacque,' with a black ribbon round her waist and black bows on her shoulders. The dress was quite plain, except for a frill at the bottom. It was short, and showed her pretty feet in sandalled shoes. On hearing her name called she stopped and turned. Loveday was in complexion like her brother, dark-haired, dark-eyed, olive-skinned, of moderate height, and graceful. An expression of gentle, patient sadness, mingled with great sweetness, never left her face. Even when she smiled and laughed, it was there, overlaid, not expugned.

'So you have come, Rose,' said Loveday. 'I thought that you were too tired to undertake a scramble.'

'I changed my mind, which is a prerogative of ladies. I am a magnet, positive and negative all in one. Your brother said so. Always possessed of two minds running in opposite directions. Your brother has been lecturing me on caprice.'

'Dennis could say nothing that was not for your good.'

'I object to his medicines. I have not asked him to prescribe for my malady. I am not his patient, but his emphatic *im*patient. Come, Cousin Gerans, lend me your hand.

Mr. Penhalligan offers me no assistance, but expects me to bound like a squirrel on to that shelf which is little lower than my chin.'

The party moved cautiously and in single file along the shelf into the bowels of the rock.

'We can proceed no farther,' said Gerans. 'Darkness palpable is to be found farther in, and here where we stand is darkness sufficient for our purpose. See! see!—the tide is running.'

A shout of satisfaction from all in the cave. A wave had entered from the Atlantic on the open farther side, and the foam, luminous like moonlight, was seen sweeping, breaking, flashing among the broken strata and rolled stones in the bottom. Then it ran on in fluid rills of light below their feet.

'How prodigiously fine!' exclaimed one after another. 'I have never seen the like before.'

'The water is warm,' said one of the young men stooping, and dipping his hand in the flood.

'It is carried by a hot current from southern seas. It brings light to-night and rain to-morrow,' said Gerans.

'We must wait and watch some more waves,' said one of the ladies. 'This is vastly entertaining.'

'Not many,' answered Gerans; 'we must not allow the tide to cover the sands, and cover our retreat, or we shall not get home dry-shod.'

'Listen to the selfishness of the men,' said Rose. 'They would forbid us a little pleasure to save themselves the labour of changing their stockings.'

'Not at all. We are considering your skirts.'

'Oh, do not care for them. We should expect you to carry us dry-shod through the water, two gentlemen to a lady, with plaited hands.'

'There! there! another wave!' was the general exclamation. A bar of palpitating white light was seen; it shot over a rocky rib, and covered it with a lambent, silvery veil, then spread in a pool, through which the flashes zigzagged like forked lightning; then gathered in a shining river of pure moonlight, and swirled past the ledge where the young people were standing, and as it did so threw out sufficient light to illumine the faces bent down to watch it.

'We must return,' said Gerans. 'This may become not a case of wet feet, but of broken necks, if we delay. The beach is not easy to traverse in the twilight, cut across with the slate ridges; in the dark it is positively dangerous.'

'Let us see one more,' begged Rose; 'we will hold ourselves responsible for all disasters.'

'The next must be the last.'

It was, however, difficult to agree as to which was the next. Small waves did not count, and there existed divergence of opinion as to the larger waves—whether they were entitled to be reckoned or not, when one flashing billow roared in, lighted the cave with phosphorescent splendour, and, by throwing its spray over those watching it, cut short further dispute.

'Go on, Loveday,' said Dennis; 'follow Mr. Gerans.' Then he grasped the arm of Constantine, and said, 'Stay behind. I must have a word with you.'

'What—here?' asked the young man whom he held.

'Yes ; here as well as anywhere else.'

'I desire wet feet or a broken neck as little as the others,' said Constantine, in surly tones.

'I shall not detain you long,' answered Dennis. 'But I have that to say to you which must be delayed no longer.'

He watched the figures of the others in the entrance of the cave, against the silvery grey evening sky, as they leaped in succession from the ledge to the shore.

'We are now alone,' he said, and turned in the dark towards Constantine, who put his hands behind his back and leaned against the natural wall of the cave.

'Well, say on.' He spoke in an uneasy, impatient tone.

'I want to know—and know I will—what is the tie between my sister and yourself. That there is some tie I am well assured. When Loveday was in Exeter, in the spring, where you were also, in a solicitor's office, what took place? Something—but what, I do not know.'

'What says Loveday?'

'Loveday will tell me nothing. She has put me off with a promise of explanation on your return. She admits only what I already know—that something has occurred, but she will say no more. She is under a promise, she tells me.

He waited. A wave roared in at the western entrance, and filled the cavern with light and noise.

Constantine moved from foot to foot uneasily.

'Well,' said Dennis, 'I am expecting a reply. Are you desirous of remaining here till the tide swells over this ledge and washes us both away? Just now you deprecated wet feet.'

'I am awkwardly situated,' said Constantine, and then he paused. Dennis waited. Nothing further followed.

'You are very awkwardly situated,' said the young doctor, putting forth his hand and touching Constantine's shoulder. 'Very awkwardly situated, face to face, in this vault, with Loveday's brother, a natural defender, and the revenger of any wrong done to her. Unless I get a satisfactory answer, I shall fling you over into the water below.'

'Two can play at that game,' answered Constantine Gaverock, doggedly. 'My arms are quite as strong as yours.'

'Possibly,' said Dennis, with constrained passion. 'But not stronger. I can hold you here. I could fling you from hence; very possibly if I cast you down you would drag me with you; if you succeeded in that, you would not succeed in disengaging yourself from my grip. Suppose we do go down together; there I will hold you till the thundering sea envelopes and batters us against the boulders, and washes us on the slate blades.'

'You need not become excited and angry,' said the younger Gaverock. 'Why should we not be friends?'

'Exactly,' answered the surgeon. 'Why should we not? I ask you to give me the reason?'

'Promise me secrecy.'

'I will make no promise where my sister is concerned. As there is a God above me,' said Dennis, sternly, 'I know that my sister is clear as this sea-water of anything that can cloud her honour. The water is crystalline, and if we cannot see to the profoundest depths it is not that the water is impure, but that the depth is unfathomable by the eye. I am not asking you because I doubt that—*that* I doubt as little as that you are shuffling and evasive now.'

'For Heaven's sake, let us get away from this place,' said Constantine. 'This last wave skimmed our ledge, and the cavern is so dark; we shall not find our way out readily.'

'You shall stay here till I have my answer.' Then Dennis seized both the arms of Constantine and pinned him to the wall.

'Let me go; I will not endure this,' cried Gaverock, writhing under the grasp of Dennis.

'I will not. Speak, or here we decide matters finally. You have had one fling to-day, and a torn coat; you shall have another, not on a gravel walk, but on pointed rocks, that will tear deeper than cloth, a fall from which you will not rise. Listen to me, Constantine Gaverock,' he said in slow, stern tones, articulating each word distinctly and with emphasis. 'I swear before God in heaven, whose eye pierces to the vault in which we now stand, that if an injury has been done by you to my sister Loveday, this gloomy cave shall receive your last sigh.'

Then a boom as the discharge of a gun, and a wall of water swept in, flashing and twinkling, with a head of shaggy light, illuminating the sides and roof; it caught the young men above the knee, and nearly swept them from the ledge.

At that moment Constantine disengaged his right hand and struck Dennis in the chest.

' A coward blow! ' exclaimed the latter. ' Is this your answer? '

He would have grappled with Constantine and cast him over into the eddying brine, regardless whether he went over as well, but that he saw before him, kindled by the mooney gleam of the water—the face of Loveday.

The girl had clung to a rock till the force of the wave was spent, and it had left the ledge. Then she stepped forward.

' Dennis!——Constantine! Let me speak. Do not touch each other. Do not strive about me ; there must be no mysteries more. The one and only secret I have ever had has burnt into and eaten out my heart. Dennis, brother dear and true, know all—I am Constantine's wife.'

Penhalligan let go his hold of the younger Gaverock.

He took but a moment to collect himself, then he said: 'Loveday, this is no place for you ; take my hand. Come out whilst you can.'

He led his sister from the Iron Gate, and landed her safely on the beach. Constantine followed.

They could hear the voices of the rest of the party who were ascending the steps towards the head of the waterfall on their way to Towan. Gerans had prudently taken a lanthorn with him, judging that the return would be in the dark, and on leaving the cavern he had struck a light and kindled it. Now the spot of yellow light travelled like a dancing will-o'-the-wisp among the black shadows, up the face of the inky rocks.

'I do not see why you should treat me as an enemy instead of as a brother-in-law,' said Constantine. 'What Loveday says is true.'

'Then why was I not told at once?'

'I was afraid of my father.'

'Constantine,' said Dennis, gravely, 'I give you three days' grace. Tell your father within those days, or I will do so myself.'

'Shake hands, Dennis, and let us part good friends.'

'When you have told your father I will give you my hand, not before.'

CHAPTER IV.

BROTHER AND SISTER.

Dennis Penhalligan and his sister walked home without exchanging many words. They were both drenched with sea-water. Constantine did not accompany them; he took the shorter, riskful path up the cliff. There hung still a soft light in the western sky, sufficient to enable him to climb the rugged way, with which he was familiar from childhood.

About an hour later, Dennis and his sister, dry-clothed, were seated in their little room over a low smouldering fire of wood.

On that bleak coast, where the atmosphere is always moist, and everything is impregnated with salt, a fire is acceptable even in summer, after the sun has set; and this was autumn.

Loveday sat on a stool by the fire, with bellows on her knee, blowing up the embers. The red pulsations of light played over her pale face. Tears hung on her long dark lashes. Her face was oval, the mouth was small, and the brow broad; her black hair was drawn back, and tied in a knot behind her head, but high. She possessed a very delicately beautiful nape of neck—a beauty more exceptional than is supposed. As she bent her head over the bellows, with her moist eyes on the fire, her pretty neck showed to great advantage.

Dennis did not speak; he was looking sadly at her, lost in a dream. What would become of him if Loveday left his house? He would be quite alone. He could not ask a woman to come and share his poverty as his wife. Besides, he cared only for one woman, Rose, and she was beyond his reach.

'I am glad you know all,' said Loveday, looking up at him, resting the bellows on her knee, and her right hand on the bellows and her face in her hand. 'I have been so unhappy, dear Dennis, in having a secret to keep from you—I felt burdened, as with a crime.'

'I do not know all, sister,' answered the doctor; 'I know nothing but the bald fact.'

She put her finger into her bosom and drew

forth a little gold ring, suspended about her neck by a blue silk thread. 'Here, Dennis, is my wedding ring. I was married at Exeter in the spring. I know it was very wrong of me not to ask your leave beforehand, and wrong again of me not to tell you afterwards, but—but Constantine begged me so earnestly to keep the secret, and I thought he intended to write home and tell all. I could not refuse him, thinking it was for a short while only. I know now that I ought to have refused, but I did not, and it has made me miserable ever since. You have no secrets that you keep from me, Dennis, only one that you have not spoken of, but it is one I have guessed for myself.'

He sighed and looked into the fire.

'Only another hopeless dream,' he said, 'like so many others that have preceded it, and burnt themselves away as fire castles into dead ash.'

'Why should you be discouraged, Dennis?' asked the girl, with her face full of sweet pity and love. 'There is not a finer person of a man than you in all the country side, none certainly with half your brains.

'Brains, Loveday,' said he with a faint sneer—'brains are of no account here. A certain amount of brain is needed to appreciate brain. Never mind me, we are speaking about yourself.'

'I will tell you everything now. I would have told you all when I came back from Exeter—but I might not. You have seen that I was hiding something from you. You know I have never hidden anything before; and it gave you trouble. Not more trouble, Dennis, than it gave me. You little know the tears and heartaches my foolish promise occasioned. I wrote again and again to Con, to ask him to release me, but he would not; he always bade me wait till his return. Now he is home it has come out.'

'Yes,' said Dennis, gloomily, ' most reluctantly.'

'You must forgive him,' pleaded Loveday. ' Poor fellow, he is so unhappily situated. You know well enough what a rough, imperious old man Hender Gaverock is. Both his sons and his wife are afraid of him. Gerans and Con have been brought up to dread his anger. Con is not, like Gerans, the heir to the estate; he is the younger son, and must shift for himself; he is quite dependent on his father. He is now in a solicitor's office, and in time will be able to support himself, perhaps in another year. Till then he is subject to the old squire, and—as you know, Dennis—there is no telling what Mr. Gaverock might do if he knew that his son had married without consulting him.'

'This is all well enough,' said Penhalligan, 'but, Loveday, it does not explain why Constantine married you on the sly.'

'We have loved each other for some years —let me see, Dennis, it is six since you bought this practice—well, ever since we knew each other we have been attached. You saw it, you made no objection.'

'I did not suppose it meant anything serious, when Constantine was without the means of living, and of supporting a wife.'

'Then he was in an office for a while at Padstow, learning his business, and after that he went to his uncle in Exeter—his mother's brother. I do not suppose he will be taken into partnership, because Mr. Nankivel has a son in the office, but Con is sure that before long he will earn his own livelihood; in time he will set up for himself at Padstow, and the family interest will bring him clients.'

'Still,' said the young surgeon—'still, I do not see the reason why he persuaded you to marry him secretly.'

Loveday sighed. 'I know it was very wrong. But, Dennis, we loved each other so dearly. Look here, brother dear,' she said, brightening, and glancing into his eyes, 'suppose you found that Rose loved you, and you had the chance. Would you stop to ask old Squire Gaverock's consent? Would you not marry her and defy the future?'

Dennis's dark complexion deepened. He turned his face aside from his sister's scrutinising gaze. After a pause he said slowly, 'Loveday, Gaverock is not my father, and—— Why has not Constantine done that very thing, confess his act manfully, and defy the future?'

'He is going to—he promised you that he would tell all.'

'Excuse me, Loveday, he did not. I threatened him that if he did not I would. I do not like his behaviour; it is neither open nor honourable.'

'You must not misjudge him. Remember

what old Squire Gaverock is. A man would think twice before he told him anything, he is so violent, so wilful.'

'That may be. Gaverock is all you say—but still the question remains unanswered. Why did you marry?'

'Because—because——' Loveday sank on her knees before her brother, threw her arms round his neck, buried her face in his breast, and said, 'We were so fond of each other. He was alone in the world——'

'How alone? He has father, and mother, and brother.'

'Yes; but his tastes, and his feelings, are so different from theirs. He has a cultivated mind, which Gerans has not; and at Exeter he had no one. He was so delighted to see me when I arrived there, and I—I was alone.'

'How so? You have me, your brother.'

'Yes, darling Dennis; a true, good, strong brother you have been. But when I was at Exeter I felt very solitary. My cousin was different in everything from me, and I was so happy to meet Con again.'

'Well, Loveday.'

'Well, Dennis; we were young things, and

both away from our relations—I from you, and he from his parents—and when he proposed that we should take advantage of the chance and get married, and spoke of his prospects, and everything looked sunny before us, I was very unwise; I consented. But from the moment I consented, and promised not to tell you, or any one, my peace of mind was gone. I assure you, brother, when I undertook to be silent, I had no idea that he meant me to keep the secret so long; I thought he intended me to hold my tongue only till he had been home and told all himself. Perhaps he did mean so —but he did not return to Towan till to-day, and I have been home for six months.'

'He acted very wrongly,' said the young surgeon, gravely; 'he placed you in a very false position. I can never forgive him that, whatever he may do to relieve you by an open declaration of the truth now. He acted in a selfish, inconsiderate manner.'

'Forgive him, Dennis,' pleaded the girl, putting her hands together. 'He loved me so very much. Do you not understand, brother, that in love one may act very foolishly and only find that out later?'

' Loveday,' said Dennis, after a moment's consideration, ' I ought not to have been left in the dark, not for an hour. Had I known, you should not have returned here without your ring, and bearing your maiden name. I shall never respect Constantine for having suffered this. A man should not allow the chance of a breath to fall on and sully the clear, bright surface of his wife's name. Constantine has wilfully exposed it to a stain.'

' Do not accuse him,' exclaimed his sister, again clasping him in her arms, whilst her tears flowed. ' I cannot bear it, Dennis. Remember what he is to me. We all make mistakes and rue them afterwards. Our judgments are at fault, not our hearts.'

Dennis stood up, folded his arms, and paced the room, with his head on his breast.

' We shall see what happens within three days,' said he. ' My mind misgives me. I do not trust him. But——' He drew a long breath. ' Is not this of a piece with all that comes on us? Everything, everything goes against us. Why was I given talents, without a field in which to exercise them? What profits my study, when the patients turn to white witches, quack remedies, and ignorant pedants? What will come of this marriage, kept concealed? No good. No good has ever come to us from anything we have taken in hand. Whatever we have set our hearts upon, if we have succeeded in securing it, has turned to mockery and misery. We have not a chance—you or I. " Man is born to misery as the sparks that fly upward," said Job. It is not true of all. It is terribly true of some. Some men are born into the world with distorted legs or spines, and some with distorted prospects. With them everything goes perversely. Providence flouts and buffets them through life. Such are we—such am I. I am like a tortured, bullied dog, driven with a whip from corner to corner, lashed from one hiding-place to another, never allowed to lie down and bask in the sun without a cut of the cruel whip across him. We see happiness all about us, but it is not for us ; ease and plenty for others, not for us ; success for mountebanks and swindlers, not for us, true and sincere. For us, corroding care, disappointments everywhere ; thorns, not flowers ; bitterness, not honey ; shadow, and no light. The light and joy of life is flowing all about us, as the luminous waves to-night, but we cannot grasp and retain any of it. Rose asked me if I had tried, and she said, " Do not wish it—it is not for you." ' He sat down by the table, and pulled a needle from his sister's workbox, then rolled up his sleeve of shirt and coat. Loveday did not notice him, she was looking into the fire.

' There are some,' he went on, working with the needle, ' to whom the world is full of blind lanes ; it is so to me ; nowhere do I find an opening where I may push my way. Everywhere am I brought up short against a dead wall. I have spent everything I possessed on my education and in buying this practice, and it scarce keeps us alive and respectably dressed. What privations we have to endure, you and I know. Is there any chance of getting away? None. Of a lightening in the horizon before us ? None. Of our affairs becoming more easy, less of a strain? None. I know very well what will follow this disclosure. You, dear Loveday, you are, in your blind love, leading to the blank wall. Old Gaverock will blaze out in one of his fury fits, turn Constántine adrift, and give us notice to quit his cottage. Where to find another that will suit I do not know. Never mind. It is all part of the writing of bitter things in the scroll against us.' He stood up and took down his powder-flask, took some of the powder, and rubbed it into his arm.

'What are you doing, Dennis?' asked his sister.

'Look!' laughed the young doctor, bitterly, and he held his arm to her. He had tattooed on it: '*Pas de chance.*'

CHAPTER V.

MOTHER AND SON.

CONSTANTINE walked home in very troubled mood. He knew that he must tell his father what he had done, and he dreaded the result. Constantine had more refinement of mind and polish of taste than his elder brother, but he had not his frank and direct character. From childhood he had experienced his father's boisterous imperiousness, which had repelled and offended him. His mother, whose favourite son he was, had made much of him, and by humouring his fancies had endeavoured to compensate for the roughness of his father's treatment. Constantine had no liking for out-of-door pastimes, for hunting, shooting, fishing, sailing, which all involved a good deal of exercise and labour. He liked to saunter in the sun, watching the workmen on the farm, or sit over the fire with a book. His father had no patience with inertness, being himself a man of effervescing energy, and he forced Constantine to accompany him with a gun after game, or with a net after fish, when the young fellow would have preferred to pick out a tune on the piano or count the sails on the horizon. When Constantine was put into a lawyer's office, away from home and its uncongenial atmosphere, he felt the relief, but the relief was only partial. It would have been full but that it was associated with work, and that work was almost as repugnant to his taste as boating and hunting. The young man was finely and firmly built, as his brother Gerans, and would have been his match in athletic sports but for that physical indolence which is so frequently associated with superior mental culture. He preferred a book to a hunt, and a morning at the piano to a morning with a gun. In music he was self-taught, and he had made no proficiency, because too lazy to practise. He liked music because it pleased without exacting anything of him. In literature he read nothing that required close attention. He read for amusement —not for profit.

His father's roughness and his mother's

favouritism had combined to destroy the moral fibre of his character—to make him selfish, shifty, and insincere. Under different circumstances he would have been other. Circumstances with him, as with Dennis Penhalligan, had spoiled his life.

When Constantine entered the hall of Towan, he found his father by the fire, with a bottle of rum, a jug of hot water, a lemon, sugar, and glasses on the oak table. Gerans was standing and talking to him.

'I have been caught in a wave, and am drenched,' said Constantine. 'Lend me a coat, Gerans; my father tore my bottle-green, and this one is sopped. I have but two here.'

'Come to the hearth,' called Hender Gaverock. 'A souse of salt water seasons a man. Here is a hot fire to dry you from without, and here is hot fire to warm you within.'

'I require a complete change,' said Constantine. 'I am drenched to the marrow of my bones.'

'Being made of sugar, you will melt. Get along with you!' exclaimed the old man. 'Gerans, give him a dry suit; and then, Con, come back to us and join in a bowl of punch to welcome your return.'

Half an hour later the young man returned, reluctantly, but unable to disobey his father. He took his place by the fire.

'Well,' shouted old Gaverock, 'what have you learned at Exeter? Can you indenture, indite, draw a mortgage, and execute a convey-ance?'

'I am learning my profession,' answered Constantine.

'And unlearning what you have acquired here—how to ride a horse and steer a boat. Eh?'

'No, father; these things are never un-learnt, any more than the art of swimming.'

'I hope not. How many honest people have you cheated out of their estates? How many have you squeezed dry as I squeeze this lemon?'

'The profession of a lawyer is as honest as any other,' said the young man.

'May be. All rogues—the parsons, the doctors, the gaugers, the lawyers. All rogues in their several ways. What!' turning to his wife—'no more rum? Only three drops in the bottle, eh ? Put the stone jars in the boat to-morrow.   I'll get more.'

'Whither are you going, father?' asked Gerans.

'Going to take Con out sealing, to keep his hand in.   You can't come, Gerans; you must go to Wadebridge Fair and buy a horse.   Con and I will run to Featherstone's and fill the jars.'

'I had rather not go to-morrow, father,' began the second son ; but he was cut short by the old man.

'Golly!' he exclaimed. 'Are you come back to play the piano and read poetry?   Not so.   You are returned to Towan to be tuned up to the proper pitch of manhood.   You shall come with me to-morrow, and prove that you have not forgotten the management of a boat.   Mother will want oil for the lamps, and Rose has been promised a pelisse of sealskin against the winter,   Do you think to win your way to a girl's heart with tum-tum and books? If you do you vastly mistake the sex.   I am sixty-five and know them thoroughly.   Stand up, Con ! Stand up, Gerans ! Back against the wall, my lady, out of my path.'

The old man hooked his arms through those of his sons, taking one on each side, and strode with them up and down the hall—he in his great boots, and his long coat buttoned back behind, and with huge strides; Gerans in his riding-boots and breeches and short hunting-coat.

'Ha! ha!' shouted the Squire. 'About of a height, all three, are we not, mother? You won't see such strapping fellows as we this side Bodmin. It is of me they draw their size and muscle and bone, as of me they take their name. There, sit down, boys, and drink. Mother, put your lips to the glass, to Con's prosperity—and may he be the man in heart that he is in figure. Ah, Con! it will be no fault of mine if I do not make as tough an old Cornish bull-dog of you as your father is, your grandfather was, and your brother promises to become.'

The evening was spent in drinking punch and talking. Old Gaverock did more of both than his sons. He belonged to an order of men passing away at the beginning of this century—now completely gone. He was stiff-necked, and not to be turned from a purpose he had resolved on, even though his reason was convinced that it was unwise. Accustomed from youth to have his own way, finding no one to oppose him, he was ungovernable in his self-will. Living in a corner of England, away from civilising influences, unreached by the rising tide of culture, among men who drank and gambled, fought, wrestled, smuggled, and were not above reaping a harvest out of a wreck, he had little of the gentler elements of humanity in him.

As he drank he became more noisy, boastful, and headstrong. To Constantine his conduct was most repugnant. Gerans was accustomed to him, laughed, joked, took his father's sallies good-humouredly, and was shocked at nothing.

At last the old Squire rose, stamped, and said:

'What, Con! scarce emptied your glass? Don't you appreciate the taste of smuggled rum punch in Exeter? Have you unlearned the liking for anything stronger than sour cider? It is time for bed. To-morrow early be up, and take with you Gerans's gun. We will go after the seals.'

The Squire was not late to go to rest; however much he drank, however merry he was, he knew his time for turning in between the blankets. He was an early riser. He was up at daybreak in summer, and before daybreak in winter, and therefore could not keep late hours at night.

Soon after he had gone, Constantine sought his room. Gaverock was mistaken in supposing that he had not drunk. He had taken more than was customary with him, to drown the troubles that worried his mind, though not as much as behoved a proper Gaverock. He undressed and threw himself on his bed, and fell asleep, leaving his candle unextinguished.

He had not been long asleep before the door was opened timidly, and his mother's anxious face looked in. She alone in the house was not asleep. She was wont to sit up last, every night, to see that the fires and candles were extinguished. On her way to her room she observed the light under Constantine's door, and she tapped. As there was no answer, she gently entered. She seated herself at his side, and stroked his disordered hair, then folded her hands in her lap, with her back to the candle, and patiently watched him. Tears were in her faded eyes, but she watched him with her whole soul, with every fibre of her heart, unable to satisfy the weary, hungry spirit of maternal love with the sight of her best-loved son.

'My boy, my dear, dear boy!' she whispered. She had not seen him for a twelvemonth, and his reception at home was not such as to make him desirous of a repetition of visits.

Mrs. Gaverock had led a life of care and pain. Only for a short moment had she known love, in the flowering of the wheat, in the first glow of youth and passion, and then her rough husband had thrust her on one side, that he might follow his favourite pursuits, which occupied his mind and filled his heart. Love is an episode in man's life, it is the epic of woman's soul.

She—gentle, loving, patient—had nothing in common with Hender Gaverock, whose interests were all external to the house. She received from him many a hard word, and much neglect, more intolerable than ill-usage.

Her youth passed without pleasure. Her fresh cheeks faded, unkissed, and her hair grew grey, uncaressed by loving hands. All her

pride, all her love, her every hope, were
wrapped up in her children, especially in Constantine. All that was sweet, and pure, and
beautiful in her humble, womanly soul had
flowed together to form one strong stream of
motherly love.

With self-devotion, fervour, tears, she had
seen her sons grow up under her eyes; she
had watched them as the seamew watches
with fluttering wings and beating heart over
her young. By degrees Gerans was drawn
from her, led by his father along his way, into
his pursuits. Gerans was pliable, and an out-
door life congenial to him. For the Squire he
entertained the most profound admiration, and
gave him unquestioning obedience. The softer
natured, more domestic Constantine was the
light of her eyes and the signet on her heart.
He was taken from her, and sent to a solicitor
in Padstow. Then she saw him only when he
returned on Saturday afternoon for the Sunday
at home. Whilst he was in this office her
weeks were consumed in longing for his return,
and in mingled delight and disappointment
when he was at home—delight at noticing his
growth, his good looks; disappointment at

finding him less reliant on her, his one and only friend.

- After he had spent an apprenticeship at Padstow, he was sent, partly at her instance, to her brother, a solicitor, in Exeter. From that time she saw no more of him till his return that day. Now, quietly, when no one was by to observe her, and Hender was asleep, unable to rebuke or ridicule her, she was able undisturbed to sit and watch with every pulsation of her heart the face of the boy she loved.

The candle guttered into the socket and went out. She could see Constantine's face no more. It mattered not; she could watch where he lay, and listen to his breath drawn evenly in sleep. His hand was outside the bedclothes. She timidly took it between her own.

When he had arrived that day he had not shown great eagerness to salute her; but then his father interposed by calling on him to unharness the horse, and this had disturbed and annoyed him. For how many, many days had she counted on his return, and when he arrived it was to disappoint her! He had gone to bed without wishing her good-night and kissing her as in olden days. She excused him again —his father had kept him drinking till bed-time, and then had dismissed him fuddled and forgetful of his filial duties.

'Mother!'

With a start she heard him speak. He was awake and looking at her. The night was not dark—a crescent moon was in the sky — and sufficient light flowed in at the window to allow of his distinguishing her, seated as she was between him and the light.

'I am here, Con! dear Con!' she said, and pressed his hand. 'I hope I have not roused you from your sleep.'

'I do not know what awoke me,' he answered. 'Perhaps it was your hand holding mine, perhaps it was disturbing dreams.'

'Con,' she said, 'you went to bed without giving me a good-night and a kiss. Therefore I could not rest.'

'Then, mother, stoop over me, and let me kiss you now,' he said ; and when she bent her head he put his arm round her neck, and drew her wet cheek down on his lips. 'Mother, you have been crying!'

'Yes, Con; crying with happiness to have you home again. You young people have many pleasures and ambitions, but an old woman has only one—the pleasure of seeing her children, the ambition of seeing them happy and prosperous.'

'Not much chance of prosperity for me, the younger son,' said Constantine. 'That is for Gerans. For me — as the paradise to which I must aspire—a pettifogging lawyer's office.'

'Don't say that, Con; it is not so,' said his mother, hurt at the contemptuous allusion to her brother.

'Whether I say it or not, it is true,' he answered.

'You may be very happy and successful if you will,' she said, speaking eagerly and pressing his hand. 'Your father has not been careless of your welfare. On the contrary, he has provided for your future, and that is one reason why you were sent for home at present.'

'How is that?' asked Constantine, sceptically. 'I thought father had neither eyes nor thoughts for any but his first-born.'

'You wrong him, Con. He is just; and he has formed a beautiful scheme for your advancement.'

'Tell it me, mother,' asked the young man sitting up in bed.

'You have seen Rose Trewhella?'

'Yes.'

'Is she not pretty? Is she not altogether charming?'

'I don't know. I paid no particular attention to her qualities of face or mind.'

'But you must do so, dear Con. She is not only very charming, sweet as her name implies, but also a bit of living, dancing sunlight; and, what is more to the purpose, worth over four hundred pounds a year. Your father is her guardian and trustee, and he has made up his mind that you are to take her and her money, and so he will provide for you splendidly.'

Mrs. Gaverock, in the delight of her heart at the prospect, clapped her hands on that of her son. He took the opportunity to withdraw his hand.

'This is rank nonsense!' he said.

'It is not nonsense, Con,' she urged; 'it is

the best of common sense.   What an excellent
wife she will make!   And your father says
that you can sell her property at Kenwyn and
Truro and buy Trevithick.   By this means
your estate will adjoin Towan, and we shall
see you every day.   Oh, Con! is not this
purely beautiful?'

'Has the young lady been consulted?'
asked Constantine.

'Oh no; but she is sure to acquiesce in the
arrangement.   Why, Con, any girl would be
proud to have you.'

'But I may not care for the girl.'

'You must like Rose.   She is so pretty, so
pleasant.   Besides, it is your father's desire.'

Constantine threw himself down on the bed
angrily.

'I cannot!   I will not!'

'But, Con, your father has resolved on it;
and what he makes up his mind to must be
carried out.'

'I cannot!   I will not!'

'Why?   For Heaven's sake do not say
"I cannot" to him — it would make him
furious.   Oh, Con, reconsider!   Do not stand
in your own light.'

'I have already done so,' answered Constantine. 'I have stood in my own light so effectually that I am out in the dark and cold. Curse it! I *can* not take Miss Trewhella and her four hundred, because I am married already; and I *will* not, for the other good reason that bigamy is punishable with transportation. I will tell you no more. Leave me. I am tired and want sleep. The particulars you shall know another time.'

CHAPTER VI.

RED FEATHERSTONE.

Squire Gaverock's boat, the 'Mermaid,' was one of which he was justly proud, as the fastest sailer between Tintagel and Trevose, that is, for her size. She was a cutter, decked, and with fixed bowsprit and mast, like a schooner. Hender Gaverock was as much at home on the deck of a boat as on the back of a horse. The only place where he was not at home was—at home, where he found nothing to do and nothing to interest him except the bottle.

About seventy years ago seals were tolerably numerous on the north-west Cornish coast. There are a good many to be found there still, but their numbers have of late been greatly diminished. Seventy years ago they abounded in the caves, where they reared their young, and in the bays they were frequently encountered—their black heads rising out of the

sea, with strangely human eyes in them, rising
and falling with the swell of the sea.

Gaverock took with him his boatman, David
Tregellas. If he and Constantine were going
to shoot seals, one of the party must be at the
helm, another at the jib, and one must be ready
with the gun for the sport.

'Got the stone jars there, David?'

'Aye, aye, sir! Strapped together for easy
carriage.'

'That is right. I'll run the "Mermaid"
to Featherstone's Kitchen—Gwen's shop. We
have drunk ourselves out of rum.'

'I reckon us had better not go so far as that,'
said Tregellas, shaking his head. 'The birds
be all flying inwards, and the water was on fire
last night.'

'Glad to hear it,' said Gaverock. 'Here is
Constantine with his brains full of city fashions,
and his nerves as slack as trade in bullocks.
Do him good to have a blow, to clear his head
and brace his tendons; and if he gets a splash
of brine in his face it will wash out the milk
and raspberry, and make his face less like a
girl's.'

'What is right for you, Squire, is right for

me,' answered Tregellas. 'You've more to lose than I.'

'You mind the jib, David; I'll tend the main-sheet and steer. Now then, Con, hold the gun, and keep your eyes open. Take heed of the boom when I say "Luff"; and don't let it knock you overboard as if you were a lout who had never tasted salt water.'

'I reckon us'll see no seals to-day, Squire,' said Tregellas. 'What sends the birds inland sends the seals to security—which proves that humans be bigger fools nor birds and beasts.'

'If they don't show on the water we'll follow them into their caves,' answered Gaverock, angrily.

'You must have a row-boat for doing that,' argued Tregellas.

The Squire growled. He disliked contradiction. He specially resented it when he knew he was in the wrong. He had made up his mind for sport, and sport he would have in spite of wind and weather.

'Wind sou'-sou'-west,' he said. 'Con, been to Featherstone's Kitchen before?'

'No, father.'

'You shall see the Kitchen whence we get

our supplies of spirits—spirits that pay no duty.'

The day was pleasant. The sun shone, and the sea rolled, but was not rough. The cutter skimmed like a bird. In vain did Constantine and his father look for seals. Not a seal was to be seen. They ran into the little coves, but the creatures were not there, neither basking on the reefs nor floating on the waves.

Nothing can be conceived more magnificent than that coast, with its crags of trap, or contorted slate and gneiss, here and there strangely barred with white spar. In the bays the gulls and kittiwakes were flashing and screaming; and now and then a red-shanked, scarlet-beaked chough went by with a call of warning. The birds were in excitement, shrieking to each other, and answering in equally high-pitched tones. The morning passed, wasted in hunting after seals that would not show.

'There they are, in yonder cave,' said old Gaverock, indicating with his chin the torn face of cliff, in which were many fissures and vaults. 'If we had only a row-boat, we could go in, and we should find them far away in the dark, lying on ledges, looking at us, or,

if we threatened them, flapping pebbles at us
with their fins. Golly! I've been hit afore
this, and had my head cut open, as surely as
if the creatures had taken aim at me with
hands. At times I'm fain to believe the seals
are human and have souls. I dare say they have
about as much as a woman. I was out sealing
—it was a day much like this—when I killed
Featherstone. Have you ever heard the tale,
Con? Well, I dare be bound you've heard
tell something about it, and all wrong. None
know the real rights but David Tregellas
and myself. Red Featherstone was a rover as
well as a smuggler. If he had been only the
latter, it would have given me a sour soul to
have killed him, though we were rivals.
Featherstone was a proper bad man. He
carried off whatever his hands laid hold of.
He had a boat, the like of which was not seen
then, but the "Mermaid" would be her match
now. Golly! I'd like to have the chance of
racing Featherstone's cutter! She was built
something the same as this. Featherstone had
a large vessel, a schooner, and with her he
went to France, or Spain, no one knows
whither. He came back to these coasts laden

with things—stolen mostly; I don't believe he paid for his goods with money. Here and there along the coast he had his kitchens—that is, store places—whither folks might go and where they might buy what they wanted, spirits and wines and tobacco, and silks and laces and china; I can't tell you what things he did not hide there, and I know he did a fine trade. The kitchens were vaults scooped out of the rocks, and cottages were built over them with secret entrances, and secret exits to the water. Very useful those kitchens were, and mighty convenient they are still. We are bound now for one, where I shall fill these jars with rum. But Featherstone no longer plies the trade. It has fallen prodigiously since his time. I spiked him. Luff! mind your head, you fool!'

He altered the course of the 'Mermaid.' 'It is an old story; it happened before you were born or thought of, before I married your mother. Indeed, I doubt if I should have had your mother if Featherstone had not first been put out of the way. The folks call him Red Featherstone, because he was fond of wearing a scarlet waistcoat laced with gold; but over it he wore a long oilskin shiny black coat. In all weathers it was the same, and he looked like a porpoise in his shiny suit buttoned over his red waistcoat. But when he came a-courting he left off the oilskin and showed his waistcoat. He was vastly attached to your mother, and I had a fancy towards her too. Of course I had, or I would not have married her. Well, Featherstone and I could not abide each other, as was natural, for we were rivals for your mother, and, by the Lord! he threatened to carry her off in his schooner if she were not given to him, so her father and brothers were armed and watched night and day when Featherstone's boat was about. One day, just such a day as this—how well I remember it, and so does David yonder! The sun was darting, a beam (bank of cloud) was over the West, lying on the sea. I was out spearing seals. Guns weren't so plenty or so good as now, and nothing like so sure of aim as a spear. I used to take one of the old weapons from the hall, a halbert with a jagged feather-like barb. I was partial to this weapon, because, if the head went in far enough, the seal could not slip away ; the barb held it. Well, as I came shooting round that headland yonder, I was close on the Watcher, which is a shelf of rock leaning with the rough broken edge landwards, and sloping towards the sea. It is only covered in a heavy sea. David and I could not see the Watcher till we were close upon it, and then, there I saw Red Featherstone seated on the sloping shelf priming his pistols. He had on his oilskin coat and oilskin leggings and long boots, and shone in the sun like a porpoise. You couldn't see a scrap of red about him. If he had his scarlet waistcoat on, it was buttoned over. But wait! you shall hear.' The old man chuckled. 'I didn't see all his waistcoat that day, but I saw some of it, as you shall hear.'

He paused, wiped his brow with his sleeve, and went on. 'When Featherstone saw me he sprang to his feet and swore, and Tregellas stayed his oars—he was that struck with astonishment he didn't know what to do. Then Featherstone shouted to me that now God or the devil had brought us face to face, and we would have it out, and settle, that hour, who should have Lydia—that's your mother. He held a pistol in each hand : one was a great brass-mounted horse-pistol, and the other was quite a toy tool, silver mounted. He held the horse-pistol in his right and the other in his left. I had no other arms with me but the old halbert; but I was not afraid. Afraid!' The old man laughed. 'I afraid! I snorted like a walrus, and called to David to pull up to the rock. I stood up in the boat and held the spear above my head ready to cast; but Featherstone was beforehand with me, and he fired the horse-pistol. He missed, for the boat was rocking, but the bullet whizzed past my head, and before ever he could discharge the second at me I flung the spear, and it went through the air straight as a cormorant after a fish, and struck him in the chest and went right through. I saw the end poking out behind, thrusting out his oilskin. That was a grand fling, that was, and I flung with such force that I levered the boat away and she shot back under my feet and brought me down. That was well for me, as at the same moment the second pistol went off—and they say Featherstone was a better aim with his left hand than with his right. When I picked myself up, I saw Featherstone wrenching at the shaft of spear to lug it out of him, but he could not,

for, as I told you, it was barbed; then it was
that I saw some of the red waistcoat, for as he
pulled at the spear he pulled the frayed,
ragged edges of the red cloth out through
the hole in the oilskin where the spear had
entered. He could do nothing with it, and
he grasped his silver-mounted pistol again, and
tried to load it and prime it; but it was all
no use—down he fell, and as he fell he
threatened me with his little pistol, but couldn't
hurt me, it was unloaded. Just then a black
boat shot out from the bay: Featherstone's
men were in it. They had been to the Kitchen with stores, and they heard the shot and
hurried to their oars, and came after me.
David and I made off then as best we
might. Well, I was somewhat curdled in
mind after that, I allow; but it was a fair
fight. Nay, it was fair on my side and unfair
on his, for a halbert was no match for two
pistols. Red Featherstone had been outlawed for his malpractices, so no harm could
come to me for having spiked him.'

'What countryman was he?' asked Constantine.

'Featherstone? He was of these parts,

and yet he was not. That is to say, his family lived somewhere up the coast just over the border in Devon. The family is respectable enough; and I reckon Red Featherstone took to roving more for sport than for what it brought him. He was a wild, wicked, restless spirit. I don't fancy the taste continued in the family. I've heard nothing of them ever since. Indeed, I do not know if the race still exists.'

'Was no inquiry made after his death?'

'No,' answered old Gaverock. 'He had been outlawed for his misdeeds. I will say that for Featherstone, he never stole anything from the people on this coast; but he was not so particular elsewhere, and I've heard he committed all sorts of depredations on the coasts of Ireland and Wales, and South Devon and Dorset, besides what he did in France. No, nothing was ever done about his death. The news got all over the country that I had spiked him, and some said it was a good job and others did not think so. And some again said that the last of Featherstone had not been seen.'

'If the man was dead,' said Constantine, '-of course the last of him had been seen.'

'Luff! Look out for your head. I don't know but that I'll tell you the reason why I say this. About a year after I had killed Featherstone, I was out on a dark night, and the summer lightning was flashing in the sky. Well, I had my eye on the lighthouse of Trevose. The light was steady enough, but what was queer to me was that every now and then something dark came between me and it, and when it did I heard a click and saw some sparks. I couldn't make it out at all till a flash came out of the West, and then, for an instant, I saw a black boat shoot past me, and in it stood Featherstone with the pistol in his left hand, and he clicked the trigger, and the flint flashed sparks, but the pistol would not go off. Ever since then I hear constantly the click of the pistol and see the sparks fly out, but I laugh at Featherstone. He can do nothing to me. The pistol must be in mortal hands to be loaded and primed to do me or mine any hurt. Then, again, one day I was in my boat after seals. Tregellas wasn't with me, I was alone, and I rowed into one of the caves near the Watcher. I got a long way in, but the seals were not there; at last I turned to come back, and as I did so, I saw a dark figure in the mouth of the cave, dressed in an oilskin long coat and high boots, standing, I fancied, on a rock that stood out of the water, and yet I knew there was no rock there, and he turned about, and I saw something like a hump on the back. I had a lantern in the bottom of the boat and I held it up, and then I had a good look forward, and I saw a pair of flashing eyes and white teeth. The shining sea was behind him, and he seemed to go up and down on the waves that rolled in, so then I knew he did not stand on a rock. He was busy with his pistol and snapped it, and the sparks flew out. Then I laughed so loud that the cave rang with the roar of my voice, and I cried, "No good! no good, Featherstone! you can't hurt me till mortal hand has hold of that pistol." I've not seen him since.'

'But how did you get out of the seal cave, father?'

'I rowed right forward and right through him.'

'How do you mean?'

'I was not afraid. I dipped my oars and

went towards the entrance, and I looked over my shoulder and saw him still there, and I struck where he stood with the prow, and then I saw sparks flying all about me; and, what was most curious of all, a spotted dog all at once appeared, and ran from the bows to the stern past me and leaped into the water again, and I saw it no more.'

'Dog! What dog can that have been?'

'Featherstone's dog. He always had such a dog. When I spiked him, the dog stood on the Watcher barking at me. He kept barking as I rowed away. Now, look out, Con! Mind yourself! There is the Watcher. That was the last I saw of Featherstone—last but once, and that was in a dream the same night. I reckon I was a bit flurried and fanciful with what had happened, and I thought at night I saw Featherstone standing by my bedside and leaning over me. I saw the red threads of the waistcoat sticking out through the oilcloth coat where the staff of the spear had made a hole, and there ran out, drop by drop, some blood. Tick, tick, tick!—I heard my watch go—then a drop. Tick, tick, tick! —then another drop. Featherstone's eyes seemed to glare into mine and through my head, and he said, " You I cannot, but yours." Then tick, tick, tick !—another drop—and he had vanished. Now, the curious thing is that, when I woke in the morning, I saw three—just three drops of blood on my sheet: so he had been with me just nine seconds. Since then I have not been threatened by him. What he meant when he said " Not you, but yours," is more than I can make out. However, I'm glad I'm rid of him. I know very well he could do me no harm. But he was a nuisance —yes, he was a nuisance.'

The old man paused a moment, then laughed and said :

' After all I do not care. Let him come again if he will. Let him try his worst. He can do nothing. Keep a good heart, and re-nounce the devil and all his works, and no Featherstone can hurt me nor mine. Look at the Watcher ! Here we are, Con, running into the bay where many a keg has been unshipped for Featherstone's Kitchen.'

The little vessel had her prow turned into a small bay surrounded by sand-hills, and with a good beach in the lap. Here the rocks were of

yellow clay-slate in thin layers : very friable and
of inferior height. The 'Mermaid' ran ashore,
and Gaverock and his son leaped out on the sand.

'Bide with her, Tregellas!' shouted the
old Squire ; then turning to his son, he said,
'Con, where are the stone jars? Sling them
over your shoulders and carry them after me
to the Kitchen.'

'Don't y' be away long, now maister,' said
David Tregellas. 'Cast your eye to wind'ard ;
there's a gale in thicky (yonder) black beam,
and us'll have to tack terrible to get home.'

'I see as well as you that wind is coming,'
answered Gaverock. 'With bread and cheese
and two jars of rum we shan't suffer even if we
reach home late and with wet skins. I like
the smell of a gale. Follow me, Con!'

Then the old man strode up the shore, and
in a few minutes reached a miserable low
cottage that cowered under a sand-hill thickly
overgrown with coarse grass. A few tamarisks,
with their pale pink flowers now blooming,
grew beside the cottage on a wall that held
back the sand from overflowing and burying
the entrance.

The cottage was one story high, thatched

with reed, built of the yellow stone dug out of the rock which the sand covered. It had a single window—very small—and a low door. Outside the door, on a bench, knitting a stocking, sat a woman with tanned face and coarse grey hair that blew about her head. She looked up as Gaverock approached and nodded.

'We have come for a supply, Gwen,' said the old man.

'You'm come right enough, Squire,' answered she, 'but you'm none going home 'zacklie as you came.' Then she pointed with one of her knitting-pins at the sky.

'Well, Gwen, I don't object to a capful of wind and the backs of the white horses.'

'Better return by land, Squire. The white horses are going mad to-night, and may kick you out of your saddle.'

'By land! Not I, Gwen, when I have the "Mermaid" to carry me. Be quick, fill me the jars.'

She took the stone bottles without another word and went indoors. She was absent for some time. Gaverock stood and looked at the sea. The day was rapidly changing. The wind sobbed among the sea grass, and tossed the tamarisks as if trying to tear them up. It carried the sand in little puffs into Gaverock's face. A haze had overspread the sky, and the sun was shorn of its brightness. Rays of vapour struck across the vault of heaven, radiating from the west, straight as sun rays, but dark; a mass of white, curd-like cloud was drifting below the upper canopy. The sea on the horizon was like indigo, near land it was the colour of olive.

'There is no time to be lost. We shall have a rough passage back to Towan,' said the old man.

'Leave the " Mermaid " here,' advised the woman, coming out with the bottles. ' Stay the night in this place. There be plenty of room, though the house don't look to have accommo- dation; and when the storm be overpast, go home in the morning. Or, if you prefer, go back by land.'

'No, no,' answered Gaverock. ' I said I'd be home in the " Mermaid "; and as I came so I return, and that—to-night.'

'Ah, Squire,' said the woman, ' you always was as unturnable as a rusty jack.'

'Take up the rum, Con!' ordered the old man.

'Here s the money for you, Gwen.'

Then he and his son went back to the boat, the latter laden with the jars of rum.

'I was not born to be drowned,' said Hender Gaverock as he slung himself on board, in reply to a question of Tregellas whether he would risk running into the storm. 'Con, take charge of the bottles; don't let them be washed overboard. Mind, as soon as we catch the gale we shall have to reef. We must keep up some sail, as we have to tack to get home, but we shall have to reef pretty short if the wind be violent.'

'We shan't pass the Watcher without reefing,' said David.

'You tend the jib,' said old Gaverock. He looked up again at the sky. The sun was behind the vapour, that was like the garment of Deianira, through the rents of which fire and venom were spurting. He untied his red kerchief from his throat, and fastened it over his rough shock of hair. That was the Squire's confession that he recognised the gravity of the storm he was about to face.

'David,' said he, 'we shall have a dirty night.'

'Dirt, sir, ain't the word for it. Say "offal"' (awful).

'David, if the wind shifts a point north, we shall do. We shall make a quick run after all, and be back at Towan to-night.'

'The night is falling already,' said Constantine.

'You mistake cloud for night, boy,' shouted the Squire.

'We had better not risk it,' urged the young man.

'To which I say Amen,' said Tregellas.

'What! afraid of a wetting as of a spill?' laughed Gaverock; and the 'Mermaid' shot out, as David, who had shoved her off, leaped on board and went forward.

Hender Gaverock had no fear. He was constitutionally incapable of fear; always in a fume with excess of energy, ever sanguine, delighting in peril, as hardy as any pilot, he despised the caution of Tregellas and the fear of Constantine. He knew his boat and could manage her as he could manage his horse. She obeyed every turn of his wrist with docility. Her timbers were sound. He knew what he had to do. He must tack to windward into the eye of the gale for a sufficient distance, and then reach away to Sandymouth, past Cardue. In Sandymouth was his harbour.

So long as he could keep up sufficient canvas there was no danger, but the gale, if it greatly increased, would not allow him to carry much sail. He must, moreover, beat outward the proper distance, or he would be swept in on cliffs where his boat would go to pieces like matchwood.

As the ' Mermaid ' leaped into the open sea beyond the Watcher, which was now enveloped in boiling foam, the wind came down on her, together with a heavy sea. A shadow like night—or like a presentiment of great disaster—fell over the boat.

' Reef away ! ' shouted Gaverock. ' David ! '

' Aye, aye, sir.'

' What boat is that to starboard ? Can you make her out ? '

After a pause, Tregellas replied, ' Don't know her at all, maister. Her looks a'most like the living black shadow of the " Mermaid." '

'By Heaven!' shouted Gaverock, almost springing to his feet, but not relaxing his grasp on the tiller, 'I'm damned if that be not Red Featherstone's boat! I know her cut. I've not clapt eyes on her these thirty years, but I know her again. What has brought her out to-night? I said I'd be glad to race the "Mermaid" against her, and though she be the devil' own boat, and sail in the devil's own weather —golly! I'll race her!'[1]

---

[1] I have worked into this and the following chapter a tradition of the North Cornish coast akin to that of the Flying Dutchman, which is found in various forms along the coast from Land's End to Orkney and, indeed, in Faroe, Norway and Denmark.

CHAPTER VII.

A RACE FOR LIFE.

'Hold the sheet, Con,' ordered Hender Gaverock, 'and throw yourself to wind'ard as ballast.
Whatever you do, but one turn round the cleet.
Many a score of boats have been lost by a
double turn.'

The wind rose to a hurricane, the waves
piled themselves up, and their foaming crests
broke against each other. The day was declining, but the dense clouds made it dark before
its time. All colour was gone out of the
sea.

Now the little 'Mermaid' proved how good
a vessel she was; she skimmed the waves like
a seabird, she danced on their crests like the
mermaid that she was. A grim smile lighted
the face of old Gaverock. He was proud of
his boat, and happy to be able to prove her
powers. She was scantily provided with ballast

for such a gale—only with Constantine, laden with the stone jars.

'Have the bottles with you, lad. Take them over from side to side,' said his father. 'We must keep on all sail we can.'

For some time he saw no more of the mysterious boat, but as he tacked he again obtained a glimpse of her; she also, like the 'Mermaid,' was standing out to sea. The little cutter leaned over with the force of the wind, the water rushed up before her bows and at times swept her deck.

For a moment the sunlight flared out a parting ray from the west, and, as the 'Mermaid' swung up a great billow, the three men saw, to port, the strange boat, as if made of red-hot metal, glowing, glaring, the sail a sheet of flame, the men on board as men of fire.

This was only for a moment. Then the black cloud descended on the sea, and night fell; but still for a while in the west a bloody streak marked the division between sea and sky. Rain began to fall heavily, driving before the wind drops that struck as hard as hail; it fell so thick that it cut off all sight of the land and of the horizon.

The sea rose higher. The gale lashed at the sea, like a savage groom lashing a horse into a frenzy of fear and fury. The wind shrieked in the rigging, the water hissed and gulped about the boat, the whole air was full of roar, in which, now and again, came the thunder and crash of a plunging billow distinct from the general noise. Already had they been swept by two or three seas, and were drenched to the skin. The water foamed over old Tregellas, who sat forward, and, pouring over the deck, rushed out behind over the Squire. The other boat was near them—so near that they could have hailed one another had they been so minded. Another reef ought to have been taken in, but Gaverock did not like to confess himself beaten in a race—which was a race for life.

Presently, however, when a furious blast sent them over so that the water wet half the sail, he was constrained to take in the second reef, and then, next time he caught sight of the phantom boat, he saw that those on board her had done the same.

'Rum, Con! rum!' shouted Gaverock, and passed the tin cup to his son, who removed the cork from one of the jars, poured out with shaking hand, and passed a jorum to his father, then drank himself, and finally handed the can to Tregellas. The spirit was needed; the three men were numb with cold, and wet to the bone.

When the rushing rain held up, the light on Trevose Head was visible; but Gaverock saw that it was now impossible for him to make Sandymouth that night. The wind was on shore and he must run out to sea, and keep well out till break of day. This could only be done by constant tacking. He did not tell Constantine or David. There was no need for him to do so; both knew it as well as he. Unless he could work out to open sea, the wind would carry him ashore between the horns of Hartland and Trevose. If he could manage to run under Lundy, he could lie there all night, ready for return next day. Fortunately the gale was not from the north-west, nor was it due west, but with a point or two to the south-west.

The phosphorescent light on the black billows seemed to the Squire to break into lambent flame about the mysterious boat that shot by out of darkness and into darkness again at intervals. By this light he thought he could distinguish the men on board, with their sou'-

westers on their heads ; but as they were all to windward, and the boat keeled over steeply, he could see no faces. Their backs were towards him, but he fancied that he saw the man at the helm with a spot of red glimmering through his dark coat and drops of fire falling from it. That may have been fancy only. In the uncertain light, with the irregular motion of the boats, with glimpses caught casually between boiling seas, in the excited, strained condition of his mind, Gaverock was liable to be deceived.

Not for a moment did the old man's heart fail him. His spirits rose to the occasion. He had expressed a wish to race Featherstone's cutter. Featherstone had taken him at his word; the phantom ship was there, come at his challenge, at one moment fiery, as if the dead man and his boat had sprung to the challenge from the flames of Tartarus, black for the most part, as though drawn from the blackest abyss of hell.

Presently he saw a mighty wall of water, as of ink, rolling on, with the blear light of the squally western sky behind it, showing its ragged, tossing, threatening crown, sharply cut against the light. Gaverock prepared to meet it, with firm grasp of the helm and set teeth. For a moment it seemed as though the ' Mermaid ' were about to cleave it—only for a moment, and then she swung up, all her planks straining, as making a desperate effort ; then a rush of whirling foam swept the deck and streamed out of the lee scuppers, as the boat lay over almost on her side. For a moment she staggered, as though hesitating what to do next, righted herself, and then went headlong down into the sea-trough, as though diving like a cormorant after a fish ; and the walls of black water stood about her, enclosing her as the waves of the Red Sea above the chariots of Pharaoh.

Whilst this happened, Gaverock fancied he heard a shout from the phantom boat, which he could not see, hidden behind the liquid mounds. Was it a cry of mockery ? or was it a threat ? He waited till the ' Mermaid ' had mounted a roller, and then he replied with a roar of defiance.

It was no longer possible to carry so much sail, and he reefed again—but with reluctance. The fury of the storm seemed to grow. He dared not reef further, lest he should lose all command over the boat.

The spray cut and cross-cut the old Squire's face, as though he were being lashed with a horse-whip. The water poured off his shaggy eyebrows, blinding him. He dared not let go his hold of the tiller even with one hand to wipe his face, and he bent his head, and smeared the brine and rain away on his sleeve.

The rum was called for, and passed frequently. Constantine suffered more than his father. His hands were numb and shook with cold. He was less accustomed to exposure than Hender Gaverock and David Tregellas. For a twelvemonth, at least, he had not been to sea. He was angry and bitter at heart with his father for exposing him to discomfort and danger. He firmly resolved never to go out with the old man again. It would be best for him to keep away altogether from home, where he was tripped up, mocked, thrust into peril of his life by the inconsiderate, self-willed old man. Now he was afraid of losing the jars of spirits; afraid of a wave washing them away. Therefore he took off his kerchief and tied the handles together with it. They were already bound together with a piece of cord; that cord he passed behind his back, and the kerchief by this means crossed his breast, holding a jar in place under each arm. Thus, when he passed from port to starboard he carried them without inconvenience. That was his first idea in thus attaching them about him, but his second was that they might form a protection for himself in the event of his being washed overboard or of the vessel foundering.

Featherstone's boat—or that which Gaverock took for it—had been unseen for some while. All at once it shot by. Then the old Squire thought he could distinguish the faces of the men on board, lit by the upward flare of the phosphorescent foam. They were white as the faces of the dead. Not a word was spoken as they went by, though the wind lulled for a minute.

The lull was but for a minute. A little way ahead through the darkness loomed on them a mountain of water, with a curling, hoary, spluttering fringe on its head. Gaverock steered direct at the billow, and the sail was eased as much as possible to help the little ' Mermaid ' over the watery heap. The wave came on as if on wheels, rushed down on them, shivering into specks of foam in all parts, on its side, as sparks blink out here and there in tinder; with a roar and a blow, it engulfed the vessel and her crew. For a moment the 'Mermaid' lay on her lee side, as about to keel over, then gathered herself together and righted once more. Gaverock heard a cry from the water. Tregellas was overboard.

'Good-bye to you, David!' cried the old Squire, and said no more. Help was not to be thought of. Then he imagined that he heard a loud, triumphant shout come to him over the water. He could not see Featherstone's boat, but the sound came—or he fancied it came—from the quarter where she must be. Constantine was now alone in the vessel with his father. They had to manage her between them. The old man could not leave the tiller. He held it with iron hand, though numbed with the cold, and with the fingers stiff, without feeling, and contracted. Soon after, again he caught a glimpse, but only a glimpse, of the phantom boat. The clouds had parted momentarily before the crescent moon, and a ray had touched this mysterious vessel. For an instant, an instant only, it shone out against the night and storm, ghost-like, as if cut out of white paper and stuck against the soot-black background. Gaverock's pulses smote his ribs like hammers. He was very angry. Featherstone, the Rover, had revisited the world and the scene of his exploits, to have his revenge on the race that had compassed his murder. He was following the 'Mermaid,' to watch and track to death the man and the son of the man who had killed him. Gaverock looked about for, and with his hand groped after Constantine's gun. A foolish desire for revenge came over him. He would have liked, next time the strange boat appeared, to discharge the gun at the helmsman. But he abandoned the idea almost as soon as it was formed. He dare not desert the tiller, and the gun was doubtless rendered useless by the water.

As the night wore on, Gaverock lost all sense of time. Hour after hour had passed, but the night became no darker; the storm, if it did not abate, grew no worse. Sometimes the clouds aloft were torn apart, and the Squire could look up at the stars and see tattered fragments of vapour being whirled across the gap, which then closed again. At times driving storms of rain came on, and when rain did not fall the air was full of spondrift.

Gaverock guessed pretty well where he was, and he altered somewhat the course of his boat. He was now, according to his reckoning, driving towards the Channel. He could see Lundy light at intervals, far away to leeward, but he had lost sight of that on Trevose Head.

Gaverock's heart did not fail him, but he was less confident than he had been of reaching home alive. He took the peril without much concern; it was what must be expected by those who went out boating in dirty weather. If he were drowned, well—it could not be helped. All must die. But he was vexed that he had not been able to keep his word, and run home to Towan in spite of the gale. Strange to say, the feeling that prevailed in him, and nerved him to battle with the tempest, was rage against Featherstone. He had dared Featherstone to race him, and Featherstone he saw would beat him, and be able to exult over the wreck of the 'Mermaid.' Not a thought did he give to his wife, to Gerans, to Rose; his one absorbing con sideration was—how to disappoint Featherstone; his one consuming ambition was—to come off with life and with an unwrecked boat, not for

his own sake, but to defeat and disappoint
Featherstone.

Between three and four in the morning, as
the dawn was beginning to lighten, Gaverock
saw again a mountain of foam before him, so
white, so broken, that he feared he was fallen
among breakers; next moment he recognised
his mistake. No rocks were there, no sand-
bank. What he saw was a mountain of seeth-
ing foam, the clash and churn of angry waves
that had beaten against each other in a cross
sea, and had resolved themselves into a heap of
milky brine, that worked and hissed through-
out its substance and over its face. The 'Mermaid' went in, and for a moment or two Gaverock and his son were holding their breath,
submerged in sea-water. When the 'Mermaid'
came out, she lay keel uppermost, and the
old man and Constantine were clinging to her
tackling and floating in the sea. Gaverock was
prepared for this. He had not lost his presence
of mind. He hacked through the shrouds on
the side, so as to allow the mast to float, instead
of working underneath her. Then, using great
exertion, he scrambled upon the keel, and
Constantine did the same.

There they sat, in cold and wet, gripping the bottom of the boat with hands and knees, covered every few minutes with the waves.

Constantine found that his powers were failing. He could hold on but very little longer. There was only just sufficient light for them to know that the night was changing to day. Constantine pulled the corks out of the jars, one after the other, and poured forth their contents, then he corked them tightly again. Would it not be well for him to pass one of the jars to his father? To do that, he must unknot both his kerchief and the cord, and his hands were too numb for this. Besides, it was doubtful whether a single jar would suffice to float a man. He looked at his father. The old man had strength and endurance in him yet, and Constantine had neither. Besides, the father had run him into this great peril, not he the father. In common justice, therefore, the risk should fall heaviest on the old man.

'Father!' he called, 'I can hold on no longer.'

'Then let go. I'll give your respects to mother.'

At that moment a great roller swept over

both. As the boat came out, Gaverock saw the strange vessel, with the dark figures in it, shoot by. Then he looked along the keel— Constantine was gone.

The old man's heart beat, not with sorrow for his son, not with fear for himself, but with anger that Featherstone should have witnessed, and be exulting over, the loss of his servant and his son.

'I will not drown. Golly! I'll spoil his sport yet,' shouted Gaverock ; and he took the great knife wherewith he had cut through the cordage, and with it he worked holes between the wood and the lead of the keel, into which he could fit his fingers, dead and frozen though they were, but still with the cling in them, set as claws.

Gaverock could no longer sit up ; he lay his length on the keel, with his red face on one side, and the crimson kerchief dripping, hanging loose round his neck—it had been washed off his head—draggling behind him.

The day was lightening. Gulls laughed and fluttered over the wreck, then plunged and shook their wings about the clinging man, regardless of him, knowing his inability to injure them. The wind was certainly abating, but the waves still tumbled, and bounded, and shook themselves into froth, and filled his ears with a sound as of a roar out of infinite space, a roar that would never end, a roar inarticulate and all-pervading. And a sense came over him of cold and weariness—of cold that no heat would ever thaw, but which was so cold as to chill and put out all fire—of weariness that would never grow less, and that no rest would ever refresh, but which also would continue the same, never becoming more acute, a dead weariness, with a thread of eternity penetrating through it. But with all, in spite of cold and weariness and noise, his will never failed—that remained unflagging, nervous, iron. Overhead, pink flashes appeared among the clouds, like the flowers of tamarisks scattered about the sky. His eyes saw neither the colour nor the light. He had no power to observe anything, he had no thought for anything, no wish but one. 'Featherstone! Featherstone! I'm not done yet, and I won't give way.'

Then indistinctly, out of another world, he heard voices, then he became conscious of something not cold and watery touching him.

Gradually he came out of his far-off realm of cold and weariness and numbness to the meeting-place of a world of warmth and action and life. He heard human voices, he felt himself caught by hands. But he clung the more fiercely, tenaciously, to the keel. For a moment his senses went, then came again, brought back by the force of his dominant will.

The 'Mermaid' was washed ashore in Bude Haven, and he was in the arms of living men.

He looked round, and saw sand-hills. He tried to cry out triumphantly, 'Featherstone! not beaten!' but his voice and his consciousness failed him.

CHAPTER VIII.

THE SHADOW OF DEATH.

On the third day after his interview with Constantine in the Iron Gate, Dennis Penhalligan walked up the coomb and over the hill to Towan. He had heard that Gaverock and his younger son had gone to sea in the 'Mermaid' on the morning of the storm and had not returned. His sister was white, red-eyed, and trembling with excitement and fear. She entreated him to get the last news for her, and relieve her alarm or confirm her worst anticipations.

On reaching Towan he saw a shaggy horse in broken harness patched with rope and string attached to a gig with torn splashboard, and wheels without paint on the tires and paintless half way up the spokes, standing before the door, with a rough boy, almost as wild as the horse, and in clothes as torn and rudely

mended as the harness, seated in the gig, flick-
ing the horse with the whip for diversion, without allowing him to leave the door.

Dennis went by into the hall. There he
saw Gerans, who held out his hand to him
without speaking.

The doctor heard a sound from the adjoin-
ing parlour like the wailing of the wind, then
words followed, which he could not hear,
though he knew the voice to be that of Rose,
and then again a fresh burst of wails. Gerans
held his face averted.

'Look at that, Dennis,' he said, pointing to
a letter on the table. 'Poor Con is lost.'

Dennis took up the letter and read it. It
was in the scrawling hand of the Squire:

'GERANS,—I've sent a boy with a trap for
you from Bude; he is to change horses at
Camelford. You are to come back with him,
and bring along with you two fresh jars, empty,
for rum. The others are lost. I'll fill them
on my way home. Very sorry to say that Tregellas and Con were drowned, poor fellows, but
the " Mermaid " is all right—came ashore into
Bude Haven, keel up, and I astride thereon; so
the " Mermaid " was no derelict, and, I'm thankful

to add, no wreck neither. Very little wants doing to her, and you and I will bring her back to Sandymouth. By the time you are here I reckon she'll be ready for sea again. So am I. Sorry, terribly sorry, about Con. Tell your mother not to be a fool, and cheer up.'

Dennis laid the letter on the table.

'This is all; you know no more?'

'Nothing but what the boy has told us. My father came into Bude Harbour yesterday morning on the " Mermaid," clinging to the keel, unconscious, or nearly so, and poor Con——' Gerans's voice broke down, and he went to the window and leaned his elbows on it, looking out, and putting his hand to his eyes, and pretended that something was tickling them.

'Poor Con,' he said, after a while, 'was washed off far out to sea. He told father he could hold on no longer—he was overcome with cold and exhaustion. Tregellas had been carried off the deck earlier. My mother!—my poor mother!'

Dennis respected his sorrow, and was silent for some time. At last he said, in a low tone :

'I am very grieved for your mother and you—very. You have my warmest sympathy. You are going to Bude now, I suppose?'

Gerans nodded.

'I want to know one thing before you leave. Did your brother say anything particular to you or your father before starting on this disastrous expedition?'

'Say anything! What do you mean? He said "Good-bye"—nothing more. He had no idea that the cruise would be dangerous.'

'I do not mean that—I mean about Loveday.'

'About Loveday!' repeated Gerans, with unfeigned surprise. 'No; what had he to say?'

'I must tell you now, Gerans. If this had not happened, you would have heard it from his own lips before to-day. I had his promise to reveal it.'

Young Gaverock turned and looked at him with a puzzled expression.

'It can be nothing of consequence now, Dennis,' he said. 'You can tell me some other time. I must be off to Bude to meet my father.'

'No, Gerans. I should wish you to know all at once, before you see him. You are regretting the loss of a brother—I of a brother-in-law.'

The young Squire stared stupidly in Dennis's face. He could not take in the meaning of his words.

'Do you not understand me?' said the surgeon. 'Constantine had married my sister.'

'Nonsense!' Gerans blurted forth. 'You are dreaming.'

'It is true. When Loveday was in Exeter, last spring, Constantine wrongly persuaded her, and she weakly allowed herself to be persuaded. They were married, but I did not know it till three days ago.'

'Impossible! My father was not asked.'

'No; your father was not consulted, nor was I. The thing was done secretly. Your brother acted in a most dishonourable——'

'He is dead,' said Gerans, holding up his hand.

'True; but when I think of this my blood boils. No one's consent was asked. They were married, and parted. She returned to me; he remained at Exeter. Months passed,

and the secret did not leak out, though I
suspected something was being kept from me.
I read it in Loveday's face. I saw it lurking
in her once so honest eyes. I taxed her with
concealment, but she would confess nothing till
the return of Constantine. Then all came out.'

'When?'

'When! Why, in Porth-Ierne.'

Gerans said no more. He looked down,
greatly troubled.

'Now,' Penhalligan went on, 'I ask
whether Constantine had told your father
before he started on this unhappy sail?'

'I am sure he did not. My father would
have been so disconcerted, he would have
spoken about it to every one. My father gives
utterance before all the world to whatever
passes through his mind.'

'You will ascertain, when you see the
Squire, whether he was told this on the
cruise?'

'I do not think Con would tell him then,
with old Tregellas in the boat.'

'Then you must tell him as you return
with him.'

Gerans shook his head. 'Don't force me

to do that—at least, not now, with this trouble on us. Father will launch out in angry words against—against poor Con; and I cannot bear that—not now, at least. He never cared for Con as did my mother and I. Con was my brother, with only a year between us, and we grew up together; we were daily companions and the best of friends. My father never understood Con's superiority—he had far more brains than I have. No, Dennis; let this lie quiet for a few days. It would heighten my mother's grief.'

'It must be known speedily.'

'Why so?'

'Because I will not have it remain hid.'

'What good will it do?'

'It must come out,' said Dennis, firmly.

Gerans sighed, and held out his hand to him. 'Well, old fellow, you think of a sister —I of a brother. Of course you are right, but give us time.'

Penhalligan saw Gerans drive off, and then he stood hesitating. Should he go directly home and tell his sister what he had heard, or should he first try to see and speak to Rose? The spell on him was too strong for him to be able to break away. Being at Towan, he must have a glimpse of her face. He knew that she could not be his, because the happiness would be too great for such as he, born under a fatal star, without a chance; yet he could not muster up the moral courage to keep away from her. He craved to see her, as an opium-eater craves for the drug; but the sight of her, instead of soothing, tortured him. He lingered at the door, with one foot on the step, his eyes on the ground. He had a walking-stick in his hand, and he scratched signs with the ferrule in the earth. 'Why should I see her?' he asked. 'The sight of her will make me miserable. But I shall be miserable if I do not see her. Why can I not tear myself away from this place and go to the other end of England? I cannot. My sister is dependent on me. All I had is sunk here, and here I must sink also.' He raised his dark eyes, full of threatening light, towards heaven, and muttered, 'Thou writest bitter things against me.'

Then, at the door, appeared Rose, looking pale and frightened, the laughter and light washed from her eyes, but beautiful, more beautiful than ever, in her pallor.

'Mr. Penhalligan,' she said, 'come, come quickly, and see Mrs. Gaverock.'

In her eagerness she caught him by the arm, and drew him after her through the hall into the little parlour beyond, that opened out of it—the one room that had a window with a southern aspect. Mrs. Gaverock was there, crouched on the floor against the window-frame, her grey hair dishevelled and falling down her back. She put her hand over her face and forehead and through her hair with a curious mechanical motion, and with the other hand pointed to the window-frame, on which were little scratches and dates.

'Con!' said the old woman, 'little Con! so high. Four years old to-day. Little Con! so high, five years old to day!' and she pointed to another notch or scratch. 'My Con, my pretty boy, my pet, my darling, so high, six years old—that is—how long ago?' She put her trembling left hand to her brow and shook her head, and brushed her forehead, and, unable to solve the question, went on: 'What a brave, pretty fellow, so tall for eight—no—where was I? I must begin again, with the first score that was drawn to-day when he is three. Con! little Con! four years, or three years?' She put her hand to her head. 'Help me! which is it? Little Con, pretty boy, four years old to-day, and so high.' She turned round, pointing, and looked at Dennis. Her eyes were dazed.

'Miss Trewhella,' said the young doctor, 'go at once for assistance. You must take Mrs. Gaverock to bed and she must be bled.' That was the panacea for all ills at the time of which we write. 'Miss Rose, I will go home immediately, and return with my instruments and a composing draught. The shock has been too much for head and heart.'

When he had seen the broken-minded and broken-hearted mother taken to her room, Dennis hastened home.

At his garden gate, before he reached the house, he saw the figure of his sister standing looking up the path expectantly.

She was able to read nothing in his face as he came up; she took his arm, and looked questioningly into his dark lowering eyes.

'Pas de chance,' he said, 'for us and for all with whom we are brought in contact, evil fortune hangs over us still, and blasts us.

Mrs. Gaverock is ill; I must return at once to Towan and bleed her.'

Loveday's lips quivered and her eyes became dim. She feared the worst. Had her brother good news he would not have tantalised her. He would have communicated it at once.

'Mrs. Gaverock has had bad news, and it has crushed her, mentally and physically. I doubt if she will rally from it. Her heart was set on one object, and—of course,' he said these words with concentrated bitterness, ' that object is taken from her. Loveday, there is but one lesson life teaches, care for no person and nothing. Be without a noble hope, without a great ambition—be as a beast, and rollick through life, and then life opens and laughs in response. Demand of it anything but what is common and base and you curse yourself with a career of misery.'

Loveday's quivering hand was in his, her swimming eyes on his.

'Sister,' he said, ' I have been told that the vulgar oyster when born has got eyes, and a faculty of seeing through them the world, and light and colour and beauty. But the silt gets in and frets them away, and little by little it loses its eyes, and light and colour and beauty are no more for it, only a base, mud-life under water. The eyes were only given it that they might be taken away, and the remembrance of light be to it a lifelong repining. Every faculty we have is given us as a vehicle for suffering. Let us love, desire, cling to anything, and that thing is taken from us! There; go to your room and cry. The blight is on you. Constantine is dead.

But she did not go. She grasped his hand tighter, and said, 'I have steeled my heart to hear this, Dennis. I acted very wrongly and Constantine very foolishly. That is over. Let the past be past. Let the whole secret remain a secret. Now it need be known to none but ourselves. I can weep for him in my own chamber; I do not care that the world should know why.'

CHAPTER IX.

THE UNSPOKEN TONGUE.

DENNIS PENHALLIGAN and Rose Trewhella were standing together in the hall by the window. The light struck in on his dark face, and Rose could not fail to notice how handsome it was. He had asked her to follow him downstairs from the sick-room of Mrs. Gaverock. In spite of her playful and flippant manner with him, Rose stood in awe of the young surgeon. To one thoughtless, without a trouble, full of exuberant spirit there is something impressive in the character of a man who is intellectual, strong of purpose or in passion, and weather-buffeted and braced by adversity.

'Miss Rose,' he said, leaning his elbow on the sill of the window, and crossing his feet, which he lashed with his riding-whip, 'I should like to send Loveday to take your place beside Mrs. Gaverock.'

'Why so?' asked the girl with a flush of hurt feeling, and with eyebrows lifted in surprise. 'Do not I care for her to the best of my power?'

'To the best of your power—yes,' answered Dennis. He did not look in her face, his dark eyes were fixed on his boots. 'But you have not in you that which the patient requires.'

'What is that?'

'Sympathy.'

'There you are out of your reckoning, Mr. Penhalligan; I am full of love and tenderness to dear aunt. She can never say of me that I neglect her.'

'You do not neglect her,' answered Dennis, 'but you do not understand what the aching heart requires. You endeavour to cheer her, to interest her with descriptions of this, that, and another, lively and entertaining, but unsuitable. You fret her much as she might be fretted by a pretty moth that fluttered over her face, or by the flicker of shining water in her weary eyes. She does not ask to be entertained, she does not want distraction. What she needs is companionship cooling as evening dew, soft as silver moonlight. You have never known sorrow, you have had no experience of the anguish of losing that about which all your heart fibres have been laced. You are incapable of helping her. The will is not wanting, what lacks is the faculty. Do not grieve that you have not got it. The faculty grows, like the blossom on the apple-tree which is beaten to make it bloom. Every bruise produces a flower, and every flower a fruit.'

Rose's clear blue eyes were on him, watching his expressive face. Her pretty lips half pouted, half inclined downwards at the corners.

'How has Loveday gained the experience that is denied me?'

'I cannot tell you how,' answered Dennis; 'it suffices that she has. You will see that the poor old lady will cling to her, but without turning from you. You tease her. You are restless, eager to be doing something for her, to stir up her mind to foreign interests. She desires to be let alone, to be wept with, to have no word spoken to her ear, but to feel the pity of a true, loving heart, speaking to her in a voiceless, altogether mysterious way.'

'You think very badly of me, doctor.'

'Not at all.' He looked up suddenly. 'Heaven knows how highly I think of you, too highly for my own happiness. But let that pass. No, Miss Rose. It is not so. Can you talk Hindustani?'

'I—Hindustani? No.'

'Why not?'

'Because, for a very simple reason, I have never learned it.'

'Why have you not learned it?'

'I have no occasion for it,' answered Rose, impatiently, and colour came in two bright spots into her cheeks. She stamped her little foot. 'What do you mean by this, Mr. Penhalligan?'

'This is my meaning, Miss Trewhella. Hearts have their languages as well as lips. You cannot converse with a Hindu, because you cannot speak Hindustani; so you cannot commune with a sorrowful soul, because you do not know sorrow. Can you comprehend how a Hindu in England must yearn to hear his own tongue? In like way the sorrowful, sick heart longs to have converse with another that can speak and understand the language of which every word is a tear.'

Rose looked on the ground, and now the earnest eyes of Dennis were on her. Her lips were curling.

Presently, with a flush of triumph in her bright face, she glanced up, and said impetuously :

' I have taken you in your own toils, sir ! You, you, who lecture me on lack of sympathy, how is it that it is precisely of you—of you that p tients complain because you are unsympathetic? Answer me that, thou Man of Feeling.'

He shrugged his shoulders and considered. Then, with a scornful smile playing about his mouth, he replied, ' Miss Trewhella, thou Lady *sans* Feeling, I will explain the riddle : for the same reason that you make a bad nurse. I am, perhaps, unsympathetic towards the sick , because I have never had a day's illness—no aches have racked my bones or nerves. I have not even had a catarrh to make me snuffle in sympathy with him who has a cold in his head. My trials and troubles have not been of that sort, they have gone under another category.'

' In what category, tell me ? ' The question was impertinent, and Rose looked at him timidly, uncertain how he would take it.

' It is useless my telling you. You would not understand me. Your life is one of unclouded happiness. You have never been in life's battle, never have received bullets and barbs of iron in your flesh which lie there un-extracted, festering, and making existence an agony.'

'No, I have not had that experience, and I have no desire of acquiring it.'

'I hope you never may have it.'

'I should be afraid to send for you, were I sick,' said Rose; 'you would dissect my fibres as callously as if you were unripping a rush mat, and cut into my poor flesh as coldly as if you were slicing a melon. I should look up into your face in vain for pity.'

'Indeed, indeed no! If you were in suffer-ing, I would be unable to touch you, not from callousness, but from emotion. And you know that, and you speak thus because you know it will set all the threads of my soul quivering.' He passed his hand over his face. Rose saw she had gone too far; she rapidly changed the subject.

'Loveday,' she said, 'is full of tenderness to the sick. You are quite right in wishing to send her here to be with dear Aunt Gaverock.'

Then she said no more. Nor did he. After

an awkward silence of a minute, she exclaimed brightly, as a thought flashed up in her mind, ' Now, Mr. Penhalligan, I am not going to let you off without chastisement. You have been hard on me, fluttering all my shortcomings, like the linen from the wash on lines on a Tuesday. I will not let you go without a last word, which is woman's prerogative; without a last touch, as in a game of prisoner's base.'

' Very well, touch me.'

' You will not be angry? '

' How can I, when you set me the example of bearing sharp instruction with so sweet an air?'

' Then be lamb-like now, Mr. Dennis, and listen to reproof. What I want to say is this. It does seem to my stupid head that both you and Loveday have gone through a rough school.'

' Yes, it is so—she and I alike.'

' And it seems to me that the same master, and the same teaching, and the same rod, have sent you out very diverse into the world.'

' Go on,' he said, looking intently at her as she spoke.

' She has been sweetened by her sorrows, and you—soured.'

He made no reply.

'I suppose the bruise does not always become a blossom on the apple-tree—sometimes a canker,' she said.

Then the door burst open, and Hender Gaverock and Gerans entered, the former stamping, shaking himself, and diffusing a chill air, a smell of the sea, and a sense of salt.

'Hullo! doctor! you here? How is my lady? Got over her hysterics yet? Here am I back, pickled in brine, and tough as tanned hide. I had a near touch this time, though; and if I hadn't made up my mind not to be drowned I should have followed David and Con to Davy Jones's locker. I held on to the keel with fingers and toes and with every claw of my will, which can grip like a crab. How is the mistress? I am very sorry about poor Con. Better, however, to have swallowed too much salt water than to be smothered in law-dust. Poor fellow! I'm as sorry at his loss as a man can be. However, that which can't be cured must be roasted and eaten, as the cook said of the pork in summer, when the pig was killed. I am sure I am as disturbed about Con as a father can be, but I don't go into hysterics. This is the way of women. Humour them, and they come round in time. I'll tell you what. If poor Con's body had been recovered, and we could have had a decent burial with cake and ale, and hatbands and scarves, the old lady would have rather liked it, and have been hopping about like a winged magpie. It is nothing but the lack of a burial which makes her take to her bed. I am sixty-five. I know women.'

'Whither are you going, Mr. Gaverock? Not up to your wife's room?' exclaimed Penhalligan.

'Yes, I am. What stands in the way? She'll be glad to hear particulars. It will rouse her out of her fit of hysterics.'

'I must beg, my dear sir, that you do not disturb her now. She must be soothed, not excited. This is not a case of hysterics by any means.'

'Don't you suppose she will be impatient to hear of poor Con, how he managed the sheet? He'd not forgotten that. I was half afraid of trusting it into his hand, but we were capsized through no fault of his. We went over and the sail was full of water. There was

no help for it. Con and I fought a gallant
fight; he ought to be here now, but is so
much younger than me that he has not my
strength.'

'You must not go to auntie,' said Rose. 'I
am about to run to Nantsillan myself for Loveday, as I only disturb and irritate aunt. Loveday is the proper medicine and nurse for her.'

'Very well! very well!' said the old man
impatiently. 'Pshaw! the house smells of
medicine bottles. Come out into the fresh air,
Gerans. Sickness makes a whole house stuffy.
Besides, I want to see the horse you bought at
Wadebridge Fair.'

When the Squire and his son had left the
hall, Rose said, 'Mr. Penhalligan, I think I
understand what you mean by the unspoken
language. I do not think my uncle and aunt
have that speech in common.'

'Mr. Gaverock,' answered Dennis, 'has so
crushed out all exhibition of sensibility in himself, and laughed and scorned it out of others,
that he dare not show his true feelings. I have
little doubt that he is more sensible of his son's
death than he allows others to see. As he has
checked in himself and in those about him

every token of feeling, he has lost the capacity
to sympathise with suffering.'

Half an hour later Loveday Penhalligan
arrived. Rose thought her looking very unwell, she was so pale, and her eyes sunken.
She asked her if she were ailing. Loveday
shook her head. She even tried to smile, but
failed.

Loveday wore a dark navy-blue cloth gown
and a white kerchief about her neck, crossed
over her bosom and pinned behind. Her hair
was plain, drawn back into a knot, and covered
by a white cap. Her sleeves were to her
elbows, where they were frilled, and she wore
long black mittens. Her features were not regular and classical, and she had an olive complexion; but there was a sweetness in her
expression which made every one say she was
pretty—some declared she was beautiful. Her
eyes were, however, her great charm, large,
deep, soft, and full of feeling; eyes into which
any one might look, and which spoke as eyes
can speak of a patient, loving, and meek soul.
Dennis saw that she did not assume a black gown,
though she had one, and he knew, thereby, that
she was resolved to have her secret kept. It

would be more precious, more holy to her, if hidden in the deeps of her faithful soul. She was not one who cried out for sympathy. She was happiest in keeping her joys and sorrows to herself, or sharing them only with her brother. They were desecrated when made public. She was reticent and retiring without being dull and shy. She never pushed herself into, or in society. She had to be sought out; but when found, and brought into conversation, her intelligence, her pleasant humour and kindliness made her very attractive. The men all liked her, and the girls were not jealous.

Mrs. Gaverock's wan, troubled face kindled the moment she entered her room. Loveday drew a chair by her bedside and took the old lady's hand in hers and kissed it respectfully.

Mrs. Gaverock said nothing, but lay looking at her. Her eyes were no longer mazed, her reason had returned; but she was very weak, and unable to speak above a whisper. But she was thinking, and thinking of one thing, her great loss; every now and then a tear trickled from her eye, and she was too weak or unconscious to put up her hand to wipe it away. Loveday saw this at once, and with her handkerchief very gently dried each tear as it welled out of the faded eyes. Towards sunset the girl was startled by the old woman putting out her disengaged hand and trying to draw herself up by the bed-post.

'Can I help you?' asked Loveday, putting her arms round her and raising her.

'Con said,' whispered Mrs. Gaverock—'Con said he was married.'

Loveday's hand that held that of the patient involuntarily quivered.

'I have been looking at you,' said the poor mother, 'and I wished—oh, I have wished so much—that he had married you.'

Loveday hesitated for a moment; her face became paler and her heart fluttered. Then she stooped, drew the old lady up in her bed; she seated herself on it, so that Mrs. Gaverock could rest in her arms, and, putting her cheek against that of the old woman, said, 'Your wish is fulfilled. He did take me.'

Two hours later Dennis returned. He found the Squire with Gerans and Rose at supper. The latter stood up, took a candle, and said, 'I will go with you, Mr. Penhalligan, and relieve Loveday.'

She and the doctor entered the sick-room. Twilight had succeeded set of sun, and then came darkness. When they entered with the light they found Mrs. Gaverock lying in Loveday's arms, asleep. Tears sparkled on her eyelashes, but her face was peaceful ; it had lost its despairing, distressed expression.

Loveday's eyes were also wet, and there were glistening paths on her cheeks ; but she smiled gently at her brother and Rose as they entered, and held up her finger to impose on them silence. Dennis looked attentively at the sleeper, and then at his sister.

'Mrs. Gaverock is better,' he said in a low tone. 'She has had better medicine than I could provide out of the Pharmacopœia.' Then he turned to Rose and said in a still lower tone, audible only to her, 'Do you now understand me when I refer to the unspoken, unwritten language ?'

CHAPTER X.

A WOMAN'S SOUL.

'Gerans,' said the Squire, 'I'm sorry your mother takes on so about Con. I can't see the sense of it. When a thing has happened, and can't be undone, accept it. Why, the Camelford and Padstow Bank failed two years ago, and I had a score of their notes in my pocket-book. I did not spread the notes out before me, and weep over them till I had sopped them to pulp. No, I burnt them all and said no more on the matter. We can't fish Con up, and, if we did, what comfort would that be to a natural man? If your mother sticks in bed we shall have to get a house-keeper, or the maids will be up to jinks. That doctor comes here every day to see her, but I know better than he how to cure her. A stiff glass of rum and hot water, with a lemon slice floating on top and a dust of nutmeg, and sugar to taste. Lord! Gerans, there's nothing like it, whether you get the shivers, or a nip of rheumatism, or have a domestic affliction, or get bad notes, or begin to think about your soul. I was cut up, I can tell you, when I was at the Falcon Inn at Bude. I was very sorry for Con, but I took the stiffest glass I could brew, and I put a bit of cucumber in it, and that relieved me wonderfully. I tumbled into bed—no sheets—between blankets, and slept like a cat in the ashes. Your mother wants rousing. I believe it's nothing but bile. I'd like to put her on horseback and send her after the hounds; get her liver well shaken, and, bless my heart, she'd be as right as Greenwich time next day, and mope no more over Con. I don't suppose Rose's habit would fit her, and she couldn't go without one. What a pity it is that the gun went to the bottom with Con! Capital gun that was; I'm only thankful that I didn't lend Con mine, but made him take yours. Lord! if it had been mine was drowned, I should have been angry. I know that gun, and it knows my hand on it, as well as Phœbus knows my touch on the reins. Gerans, what do you think of Rose, eh?'

'Rose!' echoed the young man, startled by the abrupt question. 'She is very nice.'

'Nice—that is cool praise. Say something warm.'

'Well, father, I think her very bright, cheerful, and pleasant in the house.'

'To be sure she is—full of fun, and no nonsense about her. Can't do without her now, can we?'

'We shall have to some day, when she marries.'

'What! take four hundred a year away? Not so, my good boy. I had intended her for Con, as you get Towan, and there was no salt in the box for him; but, as Con has departed, she is at your disposal. Four hundred a year in house property at Truro. I'll tell you my plan, Gerans. We'll sell this property and buy Trevithick. That will be for sale before long, and it will fit on to this estate as one nutshell on to another, and as cream fits junket.'

'But, my dear father——'

'There must be no hesitation. Stay, I'll have in some brandy at once. Upon my word, I'm low this evening with the smell of medicine, and the popping in and out of that doctor.

We'll have a bowl of punch and discuss it and your marriage together. If you've objections we'll drown them ; scruples, grate them up into the nutmeg and give zest to the bowl. It is not against the law : she is not your brother's widow.'

'Con knew nothing of this, did he?'

'No, how could he? I had no time to arrange it with him.'

'Or Rose?'

'No, I had not broached it to her.'

'But you are premature, father——'

'Premature! What a word to stop my mouth with. I will it, and that is enough. If Con had lived, he should have had Rose and her house property at Truro ; as he is dead, you shall have her and buy Trevithick. That is settled.'

'But Rose may object.'

'Golly! I'd like to see her. She object to a strapping boy like you? If I choose it—full stop—the thing is done.'

Gerans was so astonished that he could not speak. He sipped his glass and stared at his father.

'Now you know what suit to lead,' said

old Hender Gaverock. 'Lead hearts and I'll trump. I suppose there must be a little sentiment and moonshine and treacle and nightingale's songs. Girls like that, but it is not business. It is like the borage floating on top of cider cup; it gives a sort of a poetical flavour, and it is an ornament, but in itself it is nothing. Give her the blossom, but you drink the cup.'

'I do not suppose Rose cares for me, and, as for myself——'

'You can't help liking her. Besides, what is the odds? Women are women and gulls are gulls, they are all alike—one a little whiter and one a little noisier than another; but if you must have a wife, I don't see—and I've lived long enough to know—that it matters very much whom you take. They are as much alike as herrings. Some have soft roes and some have hard, and some begin with very soft roes, which become gritty as gravel in old age. You might go to Land's End and Lizard and not fare better. That is settled. As soon as decency permits, after the loss of Con, you take Rose and her four hundred, and we'll manage Trevithick.'

Then Loveday Penhalligan came in. She had been with Mrs. Gaverock, but was relieved for the night by Rose Trewhella. The Squire and his son stood up on her entry.

'Come here, Miss Loveday,' said Hender Gaverock; 'we are discussing a bowl of rum-punch, and all it lacks to make it perfect is that you should put your lips to it. Come here!' he repeated in his dictatorial, domineering manner; 'I remember when in this very hall we drank the ladies' healths out of vessels five inches long by one inch deep, and they were made of satin—the ladies' own shoes.'

'My pattens are in the hall, Squire; you may try to drink my health out of them.'

'Bring them in, Gerans, and we'll fit finger-glasses to the rings and play forfeits who spills a drop in draining the glass or breaks it.'

'No, Squire Gaverock, I will not lend my pattens for that; Mrs. Gaverock will hold me guilty of her broken bowls.'

'Take my chair, Miss Loveday,' said the old man, pointing to a leather-covered arm-chair, high-backed, by the fire.

'For a moment only,' answered the girl. She took the chair he had vacated for her, and laid her hands on the arms; the back of the chair and the protruding carved sides were above her head. She was framed in old stamped gilt leather, while the red firelight flickered over her pale face, dark hair, and large soft eyes.

'Now, Miss Penhalligan,' said the Squire, 'I am glad I have cornered you, for I want a word. You are spoiling Mrs. Gaverock. It is very kind of you to come, but don't condole with her—it makes her worse. She wants stirring up. I know women.'

'Pardon me, you do not.'

'I—I not know them!' laughed the old man. 'Golly! I have had sixty-five years' experience of them, and I ought to understand them.'

'No, you have spent sixty-five years in their society, and you understand them less now than you did sixty-five years ago. Then you might have learned, now you are past acquiring the knowledge.'

The old man stared at Loveday, amazed at her audacity.

'You think,' pursued the girl, 'that a woman's soul is to be tinkered with a slater's sax.[1] It is of too fine a nature to be touched even with the thumb. When a particle of dust enters your watch and stops the hands you hold your breath as you examine the works, lest a breath should rust them. A woman's heart is more delicate in its mechanism than that, and a rough touch and a rude blast will spoil it for ever. You know our Cornish proverb, "The earth is strewn with potsherds." It means that everywhere, in every village, almost in every house, are broken lives, lives broken by rough usage and careless handling. You would have used the finger-glasses for a jest and a forfeit, and heeded nothing if they fell and were shattered. We poor women are like these same finger-glasses, full of fresh and pure water for you men to dip your soiled fingers into and cleanse them, not for you to convert into bumpers to break for a wager.'

'Golly!' exclaimed old Gaverock. 'I called you in here, Miss, that I might have a word with you, and you are reading me a lecture. It will do you good, Gerans, I hope. I

---

[1] The sax is the short chopper used by slaters in cutting and shaping slates. The word is the Saxon *seax*, a short sword. It is in use in the West of England.

am past learning, as Miss Loveday has graciously informed us.'

There was nothing offensive in her manner; she spoke gently, almost pleadingly, and she looked delicate and pretty in the high-backed chair with her elbows on the arms, and the white frills trembling as she moved her long fingers as though playing on a harpsichord, but really in nervous fear, on the rounded ends of the chair-arm. As she spoke a light dew came out on her pure brow, and her long dark lashes were hung with molten frost drops.

'You must not be angry with me, Squire,' she said, looking timidly at him; 'if I am very bold with you it is my love for Mrs. Gaverock which makes me speak. Leave the dear old lady to Dennis and me; we will do our utmost for her, but you must not interfere and throw down the stones we set up.'

'And Rose—does she count for nothing?'

'No, I do not say that. Rose's part will come later. The sunshine will cherish and brighten when the broken flower is strong enough to bear the heat and light, but a little shade and cool and silence are needed now.'

'Very well. Have things purely your own

way. It is no pleasure to me to go into a sick-room. I'll keep away altogether.'

'Not that either,' said Loveday. 'Mrs. Gaverock will like to see you. She will expect you, and be pained if you do not visit her. When you go, be gentle, not boisterous, and not say much about Constantine. If you speak of him, speak tenderly.'

The old man rubbed his chin, then turned thoughtfully to Gerans.

'I understand her,' he said. 'Last time I went up clattering in my water-boots; I'm to go in pumps, that is what she means.' He rubbed his chin again. 'I'll shave before I kiss her. I dare say I scratched her last time. But what a roundabout way she has of saying it.'

'Comfort must be applied to a dulled soul,' said Loveday, 'like gold leaf, that is so thin and tender that it may not be touched. I have seen a gilder blow the flickering sheet into the air and let it lightly, softly fall where it is to rest, and it has fallen over the whole surface, and hidden every blemish. But if you apply it with a finger you tear it, with a brush you crease it, and leave a crinkled, ragged surface full of rents and oozing size. Long experience

is needed to lay the golden leaf; afterwards,
another hand, less experienced, may burnish it.'

Then Loveday stood up.

'It is time for me to be at home,' she said.
'Dennis will be expecting his supper on his return from his round.'

'I will accompany you!' exclaimed Gerans,
starting to his feet.

'I can return well by myself. There is no
one and nothing I need fear.'

'Certainly not alone,' said Gerans, 'now
that the night has fallen. You are so surpass-
ing kind in coming here daily to see my dear
mother, that I cannot suffer you to return unac-
companied.' He took his hat, helped her into
her shawl, and gave her his arm.

When she was gone old Gaverock emptied
his glass, kicked the logs together on the hearth,
and growled: 'She is right so far, that I don't
know women as they are in these days. Lord!
the impudence to address me as she has. This
is what comes of the French Revolution. We
shall have Charlotte Cordays here next.'

The night was not dark, the plovers were
still about, screaming, and from the cliffs could
be heard the noise of the gulls. High over-

head a flight of brent-geese went by, barking like aërial dogs.

'Loveday,' said Gerans, 'I have not seen you since I heard of the relationship in which we stand—that is, I have not seen you so as to speak to you in private. As you heard my father address you as Miss Penhalligan and Miss Loveday, you understand that he has not been made aware of that as yet. I have promised Dennis to tell my father, but I have not had a favourable opportunity for doing so.'

'I do not see occasion for it,' said Loveday. 'Let it be buried in the past.'

'Poor dear Con acted very wrongly by you. He ought to have been more considerate of——'

'Not a word against him!' interrupted the girl. 'As you have not told Mr. Gaverock, let the story remain untold. I ask nothing from him; I acted wrongly and I must bear the consequence. I shall always have your regard, I trust?'

'Always, always, dear Loveday!'

'That suffices. Mrs. Gaverock knows, and is happy in the knowledge. There is really no occasion why your father should be troubled by being told what has taken place. It is in the past. It can do no good to repeat it, and I know he would be very indignant if he heard it.'

'Well, sister, his anger would blow away in a week or two.'

'In that week he would say words which would hurt your mother and me where our hearts are most tender, and the wounds would not heal for years.'

'It is but right, Loveday, that your connection with the family should be known and acknowledged.'

'If it were, reflections would be made on poor Constantine for not having himself made it known and having exacted acknowledgment months ago.'

'That is true, but your honour is more to be considered than my brother's memory. I cannot in conscience submit.'

'You do not understand a woman's soul,' answered Loveday, quietly. 'It is of that nature that it will endure anything rather than that the slightest injury should be done, even to the memory of the man she loves. But do not be troubled on that score. My secret is safe in the hands of yourself and your dear mother. In such good kind hands let it lie. Good-night, brother Gerans; I am at my gate. Think better of women and deal more tenderly with their fluttering hearts than does your father with his experience of sixty-five years.'

CHAPTER XI.

A STUDY IN DRAWING.

PRAXITELES is said to have sculptured an Eros which seemed to laugh, but which, when the eyes of the figure were bandaged, seemed to be grave, even stern. Rose Trewhella's eyes danced with the ἀνήριθμον γέλασμα of the sparkling summer sea, but there was sufficient decision in the lines of her mouth and in the moulding of her nostrils to show that there were the elements of a firm character in her, undeveloped—a potentiality and a promise. At present she was frivolous, careless, pleasure-loving, without a perception of the seriousness of life, without a thought of dangers that might menace her unless watched against, of pitfalls among which she might be drawn by her own thoughtlessness.

She had been spoiled as a young girl, and had grown to be wayward and exacting. Her

father had been careless and good-natured. She
had been petted by him, and flattered by his
fox-hunting friends. She had associated very
little with girls of her own age. Her governess
had been ruled by her, she had fixed her own
hours of work and studies. Her education had,
therefore, been desultory.

But there was good, sterling good, in the
mine of her heart, overlaid with much worthless stuff. She had obtained whatsoever she
wanted from her father by coaxing or by sulk-
ing; and she supposed that these two recipes
were infallible, and would suffice her to get all
she wanted out of other men.

When Gerans returned from Nantsillan, he
found Rose in the hall with his father. She
had left Mrs. Gaverock when the old lady went
to sleep. The Squire liked Rose; she joked
with him, teased him, showed him a certain
amount of deference, and submitted to his authority. Rose sat in the chair recently vacated
by Loveday, and presented the most marked
contrast to her. Her hair was tossed into a
tangle about her head, like floss silk; it was
fair and golden; in it was a fine strip of white
cambric, but whether tying the hair or en-

tangled in it, inextricably, could hardly be told. It was like a ribbon we sometimes see woven into a bird's-nest among the twigs. Her cheeks were bright with colour, and her blue eyes sparkled with mischief.

Directly Gerans entered she attacked him.

'You have had a *very* pleasant walk in the twilight, cousin, I am sure.'

'I have seen Miss Loveday home.'

'You need not tell me that. I got a glimpse of you starting arm in arm, and thought you made a pretty pair.'

Gerans coloured.

'It would have been unmannerly to have let her return to Nantsillan unescorted.'

'Gerans the gallant! Gerans the courtly! What it must be for a young damsel to have such a knight to attend her! You seemed to be in close conference. I suppose the subject was *most* interesting—to yourselves.'

Rose saw that Gerans was uncomfortable, and so she went on mischievously. She was not jealous of Loveday, but she liked tormenting Gerans, who was not agile of mind to evade or parry her thrusts.

'Now,' said she, going up to him, and look-

ing slyly into his eyes, 'what was it all about?
Tell me, if you can, the topic of your talk.'

Gerans was confused, and stammered an
incoherent reply. Afterwards, when he was
alone, he thought, 'How stupid of me! I
should have answered that we were speaking
of poor Con. But that is the way with me; I
never hit on the right thing to say till it is too
late to say it.'

The old father's suspicions were roused, and
he looked at his son with mistrust. When
Rose had left the room he said roughly,
'Gerans, I will have no foolery with Miss
Loveday. I have told you my mind. You
know what is expected of you. As for Mistress
Malapert, she is an impudent hussy, and I dislike her. Prodigiously daring to tell me that I
know nothing of women! What is her age?
Twenty-one, I suppose. Been a woman three
years, only a girl before, and I have had sixty-
five years of experience of the sex. What was
that she said of a woman's soul? A fine piece
of mechanism not to be breathed on. That is
flam! It is like a peacock's tail. Whirr!
spread to blaze and dazzle you with its glitter
and colour and eyes, then draggled in the wet

and mud, and dropping a dowdy feather in the
dank grass. Pshaw! It is a thing of show.
I not know women!

> A woman, a dog, and a walnut tree,
> The more you whip 'em the better they be.

Mind you this, Gerans, I will not allow you to
think of Loveday. As poor Con has gone to
the bottom of the sea, you must take Rose.
That is a settled matter. As for Mistress
Loveday, God bless my soul! we should fight
if she and I were in the house together a week.
I cannot stand opposition, leastways from a
woman.'

Next day Rose's mood was changed. She
would not speak at early dinner, and went into
the parlour to sit by herself, with her hands in
her lap, looking out of the window. Gerans
followed her.

She did not turn her head when he opened
the door, nor when he came across the floor to
her. He placed himself in the window, with
his back to the light, and looked at her. Her
lips were pouting, and her brows contracted.

'Are you unwell, Rose?'

'Oh dear, no, Mr. Gerans Gaverock. But

it does not matter; no one here cares how
I am.'

'Why do you say that? You surely know
how highly we all regard you.'

'You regard me so highly as the lark, that
is so high that it is altogether lost to sight,
Master Gaverock.'

'You used to call me Cousin Gerans.'

'It was a mistake. You came to consider
me as a cousin, one on whom the common
courtesies of life, when expended, were wasted.
Look on me rather as an acquaintance, and
then I shall receive proper treatment.'

'But what have I done to offend you?'

'Oh, nothing,' said Rose, rising and settling
her skirts and sitting down again. 'That
creeper should be cut; it is trailing over the
window.'

'I will see to the creeper another time.
Why are you cross with me?'

'Cross! You are rude; a lady is never
cross. But this is the way with you men—you
charge us with having the vapours, and do not
consider the occasion, which is to be found in
yourselves.'

'But what have I done to offend you?'

'Nothing,' answered Rose, looking him coldly in the face.

'Then why are you so dissatisfied?'

'I am not dissatisfied, because I have expected nothing. I am dissatisfied when taken to a wax-work, and see what poor figures are within the booth, different from the painted promise without, but I am not dissatisfied where nothing has been promised and nothing performed.'

Gerans was perplexed. He looked at her with puzzlement in his brain, and said, humbly, 'I don't know what you want; but I do know that we are all your dutiful servants, waiting on your wishes.'

'I have been wanting to wind a skein of wool for a week, and no one has offered me his hands on which to spread it.'

'But, surely, Miss Rose, you had only to express the desire, and my father or I would have flown to offer you help.'

'With the eagerness you flew yesterday to offer it to Loveday. I warrant me she had not to ask for your arm. You forestalled her wish; you pressed your arm on her. Was it not so?' Gerans was confused. 'Whereas poor I—I must wait a week, and ask outright for help, or a hand is not held out to me.'

'Surely, Miss Rose, this is unreasonable——'

She interrupted him with an assumption of anger, and started back in her chair. 'Unreasonable, am I, and cross-grained, crabbed, spiteful; what next? Really, Mr. Gerans Gaverock, the Master of Manners does not come round these parts, or I would pay to send you to be schooled by him.'

'I did not know you wanted any wool winding, or I would have been proud and happy——'

'You did not see that I was working a border of a running scroll for the drawing-room fire-mat. You did not give sufficient thought to consider that my little ball of red wool was drawing to an end. You have no eyes for my necessities. They are engrossed by Miss Penhalligan, I take it.'

Gerans coloured.

'You deal very hardly with me,' he said, penitently. 'I assure you I am not thinking of Miss Loveday in the way you suppose.'

Rose laughed merrily and mockingly. 'Mr.

Gerans, I do not want your assurances. I am too supremely indifferent to you to be made a confidante of your partialities.'

'Where is the wool?' asked Gerans, desperately.

'Here. Are you going to be polite?'

Gerans held out his hands.

When a young and pretty girl has got a man fast with a skein about his fingers, which she is winding in a ball, she has him completely in her power. He is conscious that he is in a position somewhat ludicrous and not manly. He has to raise one hand and depress the other in obedience to the beck of her finger. Whatever she may say he cannot escape. He is her captive for a quarter of an hour. The man may have splendid abilities, but he is unable to exercise them: his mind must follow the run of the thread forwards and backwards, and he cannot think of anything else. At the same time the girl is winding mechanically, and exercising all her wits to torment or coquet with the victim.

Gerans, honest-hearted, slow of thought, spent a very uncomfortable twenty minutes thus tied; he was in continual fear of entangling the threads. They did catch occasionally, and, when they caught, Rose was obliged to come close to him, make him hold up his hands, whilst her golden head turned and dipped about, very close to his, and her delicate, fragrant hands passed in and out between his palms, turning the ball this way, then that—he could almost have thought she was purposely entangling the wool, had he possessed sufficient guile to suppose it.

When a young girl holds the ball, and a man has the skein, there is a link of connection established between them—a wire of communication is drawn from one battery to another. The days of which we write were not those of the electric telegraph ; but a telegraph of some sort, conveying a series of messages, was set up whenever a young lady asked a young gentleman to hold the wool for her while she unwound. A heart was at each end, a battery and a registering table together. What touches, what tremulous quivers, what strange little tweaks the ball-spinner is able to send along the thread to the hands of the skein-holder! It happens that the threads of the skein pass over the most sensitive portion of the hand, between the fore-finger and the thumb, and this registers all the little defiances, and trembling entreaties, and quivering appeals, and bold assaults of the ball-winder, and delivers them all, sealed from every eye, direct to the heart of the skein-holder, who cannot refuse them, so engrossed is he in his mind on the vibration of the thread over his hands.

When at length the end of the wool was drawn slowly, almost reluctantly, off his left hand, and he recovered the possession, first of the right, then of the left, Gerans was in a bewildered condition, not very sure that he retained possession of his heart—whether that had not also been wound away at the tail of the worsted and secured by Miss Rose.

'Thank you so *very* much, Cousin Gerans,' said she, raising her blue eyes and looking at him with an appeal for mercy in them. 'I am sure I have been most exacting.'

'Not at all. I like it.'

'Do you now?' A roguish twinkle came into her eyes, and dimples formed at the corners of her mouth. 'You like being made to take the place of the backs of chairs. How good of you to say so; but you do not mean it?'

'I am always ready to do anything for you, Rose.'

'Then you will not be cross with me any more?'

'I cross!' He was justly astonished.

'I suppose that no one knows his own faults; certainly no man will confess his—leastways to a woman. Yet, you have been very cross and peevish with me. I could scarcely bear it.' Her voice shook, as the thread had shaken in her fingers lately.

'You have been very much mistaken, Rose.'

'No, I have not. Trust a girl to read the moods of those she is with. She opens in the sun, and shivers and droops when there are clouds in the sky.'

'I was unaware of it. I am sure you misunderstood; I could not be cross with you.'

'You want some one always at your side to tell you of your faults, and bid you correct your blunders.'

'Oh, Rose! if you will execute that office for me, it will be a delight to me to mend my ways.'

'You would not believe me when I told you you were erring.'

'I would believe anything from those lips.'

'Then you would have your faith sorely tried,' said Rose, with a laugh, 'for I say one thing this moment and another thing that. Hark! Mr. Gerans Gaverock, there comes Dennis down from your mother's room.'

'Dennis!'

'You did not hear him go up, you were so engrossed in the skein. I did; and now he returns. I must positively see him!' Then she ran into the hall, and was followed by Gerans with heightened colour.

'How do you do?' said the girl, stepping up to the doctor. 'How is Mrs. Gaverock? Why has not Loveday been up to-day? Is it the drizzle that detains her? What a day it is!—rain squeezed through a hair sieve, neither falling nor rising nor driving, but floating in the air.'

'I have found my patient slowly mending,' said Penhalligan. 'She must have the same treatment—must be kept very quiet.'

'And Loveday? Is she coming here?'

'Not to-day. She is not very well, and there is no necessity.'

'Then I will go to her. Mr. Penhalligan,

will you hold an umbrella over me? I have
found this day more dull in the house than it
can possibly be outside, and so I will venture
forth. Mr. Gerans has informed me that I
have the vapours. I will take my vapours out
into the general fog. May I ask you, Mr.
Penhalligan, to wrap that cloak round me? I
am clumsy with my overshoes: is it asking too
much of you to desire that you would put
your hand to help to slip them over my feet?
Thank you ; you are very kind. I dare say I
shall not find it *quite* as dismal when I am out
of Towan as the day has seemed to me looking
forth from the windows. You will lend me
your arm, and be careful that the drip of the
umbrella does not go down my back—will you
not, Mr. Penhalligan?'

When they were gone Gerans took up the
bellows and began to blow the log that was
smouldering on the dogs in the fireplace.

'Well, Gerans,' said his father, 'how are
you getting on?'

'Middling,' answered the young man. 'The
log is green, and will not blaze.'

Old Gaverock snatched the bellows from his
hand, and sent puffs from the nozzle on his son.

'Oh, you green stock!' he shouted. 'It is you that do not kindle. When I was a young man it was quite other. You are slow and sleepy, without spark and crackle. What do you mean by allowing Penhalligan to carry your mistress off to Nantsillan? You be on the alert, or he'll take her away altogether—and then we shall lose Trevithick. Gerans, I went all over Trevithick yesterday, and I'll take you there to-morrow. We must have it. It comes alongside of Dinnabol Farm, as if made to run with it. At Dinnabol the sheep get the rot because of the wet clay; let them have the healthy moor of Trevithick to run on, and you can fatten at Dinnabol. In the autumn the mischief is done in the clay lands, and at Dinnabol we have no sound runs for the sheep. Gerans, we must and we shall have Trevithick.'

'I don't suppose Rose cares for me,' said Gerans, in a depressed mood, which showed itself by his tone of voice. 'If she had any regard for me she would not tease me so cruelly.'

'You are a fool, Gerans. I know she likes you.'

The young man shook his head; he was

very red in the face, annoyed with Rose, angry with Penhalligan.

'I tell you she does,' pursued his father. 'That Mistress Malapert dared to say I knew nothing of women—I with my sixty-five years' experience. I can see through Rose as if she were a tumbler of water dipped out of the Atlantic. She is drawing you, Gerans. I know it *because* she teases you.' The old man began to sing—

> Phyllis is my only joy,
> Sometimes forward, sometimes coy.

'She was kind to Dennis Penhalligan and cruel to me,' said Gerans.

'My good fool!' exclaimed the old man, 'that is all part of her play. Run after her. You are not going to let that Doctor Sawbones walk with her to Nantsillan and walk back with her as well?'

'She might not like my pursuing her.'

'Nonsense! she wants you to run after her.'

He forced his son out of the house, then he reseated himself in his armchair, and burst out laughing. 'And so Mistress Malapert said I did not know women!'

CHAPTER XII.

NANTSILLAN.

Rose Trewhella had hardly got out of sight of Towan before she let go her hold of Dennis's arm, and said, 'Mr. Penhalligan, I do not think that the umbrella is of the slightest use against the mist. Moreover, there are so many puddles which I must skip over or circumvent that I can do better for myself if I walk unassisted. How long have you known my cousin Gerans? Have you been friends from boyhood? You know he is not really my cousin; indeed, we are no relation whatever, but it would sound too unfriendly to call him Mr. Gerans, and too familiar to call him Gerans, so I split the difference and designate him cousin. I think him very nice, do not you?'

'Whoever commends himself to you needs no praise from me,' answered Dennis.

'Now, Mr. Penhalligan, this is one of your

stiff, set phrases, fine sounding and evasive. I
want your *real* opinion of him.'

'I think that he is truthful, sincere, and
kind-hearted.'

'I am glad you think that. But he is
stupid and slow ; you will allow that ? '

'He will mend in time.'

'When ? '

'When weaned.'

Rose looked round and laughed. 'What
do you mean ? '

'At present he thinks, sees, hears, smells
through his father's organs, and acts as his
members. When the old Squire dies, or when
Gerans marries, he will cut his teeth. He has
not his brother's quickness, but such docility
and honouring of a father must deserve him
length of days in the land—denied to the less
submissive younger brother.'

Rose bit her lip, and looked out of the
corners of her eyes at Penhalligan. He was
walking with his head down ; his dark face
was wet with the fog, his lips were set, and his
brow was gloomy.

'I am sorry for Loveday,' said Rose.
'What is the matter with her ? '

He moved his shoulders uneasily. 'Nothing to signify. She cannot go every day to Towan. There are home duties. We do not keep a servant. This is our washing day.' He coloured as he spoke.

'Why did you not say so, instead of pretending she was ill? I shall be in the way. I shall go back.' She stood still.

'No, no, Miss Trewhella,' he begged; 'do not return. Pray come on. Loveday will be so delighted to see you—so honoured by your crossing our mean threshold.'

'Why did you say she was ill when she was not?'

'Because,' he answered, 'I am a moral coward, and I was ashamed to admit that she had the scrubbing and the ironing to do. Poverty is dishonour.'

'Not at all; poverty is honourable.'

'Then why are we ashamed to confess it?'

'We are ashamed to be thought religious and temperate and thrifty; and out of the same perversity we are ashamed to be thought poor. How long have you known Gerans?'

'For five or six years— ever since I have been here.'

'Which did you like best—Gerans or his brother who is dead, Constantine?'

'I preferred the society of the younger. He often came to us. He was musical, so am I, and I have a pianoforte that belonged to my mother.'

'You play! How clever you are!'

'A surgeon need be nimble of fingers; and practice on the keys is good schooling for delicacy of touch on the human nerves. Here we are at my cottage.'

'You are sure I shall not be in the way? I will just speak to Loveday and run away.'

'I will accompany you home if you must return.'

'Not so. I can go back to Towan by myself. But perhaps Gerans will come to fetch me. I am teaching him to be polite to ladies.'

So she went in.

The cottage was small; it consisted of a reception room or hall, small, floored with slate, and low. Also of a tiny parlour at the side, and a surgery. The parlour was unfurnished, and was used as a work-room. The brother and sister sat in the hall. This room had whitewashed walls; against them were hung the surgeon's diploma, a sampler worked by Loveday's mother when a girl, giving the letters of the alphabet, the numerals, a tree, a flower, and a bird all of the same size.

On the chimney-piece were two good old china vases, relics of better days, and against the wall away from the door was a piano, another relic of a time when the Penhalligans were better off. Before the hearth was a rug made of scraps of cloth woven into a piece of canvas—warm, but plain. Muslin curtains hung over the window. Everything in the room and about the house was very plain, but clean and in excellent order. The garden beds within the wicket-gate were carefully attended to and free from weeds. The flowers in them were common, but bloomed freely, in gratitude for the care shown them. Against the walls of the house were a jessamine and a monthly rose that was a free bloomer. In the hall, although everything was plain, yet an air of snugness and of beauty was afforded by the abundance of flowers and leaves wherewith it was adorned. In saucers were blackberry leaves of every shade between lemon yellow and carmine, beech leaves of warm copper hue, pink dog-

wood leaves, and the transparent crimson berries
of the wild guelder rose, pale blue Michaelmas
daisies, clusters of rose-hips, feathery traveller's-
joy, sprigs of crane's-bill still flowering, blue
borage, graceful rainbow-coloured carrot leaves,
delicate white-veined arrow-headed blades of
ivy, beautiful grasses—the table, the chimney-
piece, the window, the whatnot, were adorned
with posies, each of which was a study in
colour, all picked, sorted, settled in their
glasses by the skilful fingers of Loveday. Bare
of furniture, lacking in ornament the room
might be, but it was scrupulously clean, and
brightened by these charming clusters of
autumn leaves and flowers.

Rose had no time to look round before
Loveday herself came to her from the parlour,
with colour glowing through the olive skin of
her cheeks, and her dark eyes shining with love
and pleasure. She held out both her hands to
Rose, and Rose saw that they were crinkled
with immersion in hot water. Loveday wore a
thin cotton gown, and had arms bare from the
elbow, very white, streaked with pretty blue
veins.

Rose caught Loveday almost boisterously in

her arms, and kissed her on both cheeks and on her lips.

'That designing brother of yours pretended you were seriously ill, and brought me here to nurse you. In reality he desired the pleasure of my society; he was tired of the dull walk alone in the mist. Now you are busy, and I suppose I shall be in the way. Yet I must detain you from your work for three minutes. Oh! it is insufferable in Towan. Guardy says to his son, "Gerans, good boy, trot into the parlour and talk to Rose," and in the tame fellow trots. Presently the old gentleman puts in his head at the door and says, "Gerans, good boy, that will do, come here!" Then the tame fellow goes pit-a-pat back to his place at the old man's heel. Next the Squire says, "Curl yourself up in a corner by the fire, and I give you leave to snore." Then the docile creature curls up and snores. Presently the father takes the bread and cuts it up, and says, "Gerans, sit up prettily and beg," so up he sits on his hind feet and holds his front pats before him— so!' She imitated a dog begging. ' "Snap!" says Mr. Gaverock, and snap goes Gerans. It is really wonderful how well trained the creature is. Is it not so, Mr. Penhalligan?' asked Rose, turning sharply round and confronting Dennis.

Loveday took Rose by the hand, and drew her into the parlour and shut the door.

'Do not say these sharp things, dear,' she said in a gentle tone. 'Gerans is very good. Look for the excellences in people, not for their weaknesses, and you will be the happier.'

'I have not spoken half as sharply as your brother,' said Rose, in self-defence. 'I give Gerans credit for being a well-trained poodle; Mr. Penhalligan said he was an unweaned baby.'

'I am sorry Dennis said that; it is not true.'

'Of course you take up the cudgels for Gerans Gaverock.' Rose pouted as she spoke. 'He is so civil to you, and forestalls all your wishes.'

Loveday's clear frank eyes rested on the twinkling blue eyes of Rose, and the latter fell before the steady gaze. 'Dear Rose,' said Loveday, 'Gerans is nothing more to me, can be nothing more to me, than a kind and trusted— almost brother. I shall, I can, think of him in no other light, so give way to no romantic fancies. Gerans is honourable, straightforward,

and simple-hearted. We have all our weaknesses, you as well as he—I most of all. Two
men look on the same face and draw it; the
one makes a beautiful portrait, the other a cari-
cature. The one leaves out of sight all that is
gross, and sordid, and common in the face; he
paints the soul—as it might and may be—
shining through the features as through a figured
globe. The other knows nothing of soul, sees
no ideal, believes in none. He grasps everything that is ridiculous, mean, and transitory in
the face, and delineates that. You must look
at mankind as either the painter or the carica-
turist. It is best for us to take the higher
platform.' After a short pause: 'Will you help
me, dear Rose?'

Rose looked round the parlour; it was
wholly unfurnished. The Penhalligans used
only the hall. One room sufficed them, and
Loveday did her ironing in the parlour. The
long deal table was covered with linen, a fire
was in the grate, and irons stood around it,
becoming heated.

'Rose, I am ironing my brother's collars
and shirt-fronts. Will you goffer these frills for
me?'

'My dear Loveday!' exclaimed Rose, 'I wish with all my heart I could; but I never did anything useful in all my life, except wool-work.'

'And that is very useful. I wish I had time to do some.'

Rose's heart fluttered and her eyes danced. 'Loveday, you darling! Will you? Oh, don't say me nay!'

'How can I till I know what you want?' said the other, laughing.

'I have begun a mat—that is, the border for a mat to go before the fire. It is very pretty; the ground olive-green with a broad scroll over it of folded ribbon, shaded from red to white. I began it three years ago, and I do a little from time to time. Now I will attack it like a dragon if you will accept it from me and use it for your parlour mat when you fit up this room. Why have you not furnished it?'

'We are waiting for our ship to arrive,' answered Loveday, 'and Nantsillan Cove is so dangerous with reefs that our ship has not yet ventured in.'

'But,' began Rose, looking round her

with wonder, 'why does not your servant do this?'

'Because our servant is a little girl of twelve, and she would probably spoil the things.'

'Does she cook your dinners and make the bread?'

'No; I am cook and baker.'

'She cleans the rooms and makes the beds?'

'No; I am housemaid.'

'And the garden? Who attends to that?'

'I am gardener.'

'But Mr. Penhalligan's horse? Surely you are not groom also?'

'No, that I am not; my brother is his own groom.'

'This is very strange to me. And your dresses? And the linen? Are you also dress-maker and scouring maid?'

'Yes, I am.'

'Then,' said Rose, 'I am a very useless creature in the world. I cannot understand you. You work like a common woman, and yet you look always like a lady.'

'Am I not a lady?' asked Loveday, with a quiet smile.

Rose in reply threw her arms round her and kissed her again.

'How good!—how very good you are!' she said with a gush of love and enthusiasm. 'I wish—oh! I wish I were like you!'

Loveday shook her head and went on with the ironing whilst she talked, glad, perhaps, to be able to hide her face by bending over her work.

'No, dear, I am not good. I have committed grave faults; I have done things both foolish and wrong, for which I shall grieve all my days, the shadow of which will always hang over me. I have had more experience of life than you, that is all, and I am oldened by it beyond my years.'

'There is Gerans!' interrupted Rose, starting, as she saw his head pass the window. 'I thought he would come. I suppose his father has sent him. I will charge him with it.'

'Prithee do not,' entreated Loveday, laying aside her work and going up to her. 'You will wound him—that will be the result; and is that a result to be desired?'

'He should come unprompted.'

'Perhaps he has; possibly not. Does it

matter? He wanted to leave, and Mr. Gaverock suggested that he should. Two hearts
felt kindly towards you instead of one. You
should be pleased to have it so. Now, one word
with you before we go into the next room to
them.' Loveday's face became distressed, and
her hand clasped Rose's arm nervously. 'Do
not play tricks with my brother. I know you
mean no harm, but Dennis is unable to bear
trifling. He takes everything seriously, too
seriously. You remember the fable of the frogs
and the boys who threw stones at them. "What
is fun to you," said the frogs, " is death to us." '

Rose's tell-tale mouth twitched, the lips
pouted, but the corners went down ; she was
half disposed to defiance, half to cry.

'We will detain both you and Mr. Gerans,'
said Loveday, 'and have tea ; then Dennis and
I will do our best to amuse you with music.'

'Oh, that will be prime !' exclaimed Rose,
laughing. 'But how about the ironing ? Is
Mr. Penhalligan to go limp-collared to-morrow
because we are here ? '

'Leave that to me. We shall have a pleasant
evening.'

CHAPTER XIII.

A QUIET EVENING.

LOVEDAY went out of the parlour at once to meet and welcome Gerans, and invite him in to a dish of tea. 'You will excuse me,' she said smiling, 'if I run away for a few minutes and put off my work-a-day for my holiday gown. It is a holiday indeed for us to entertain friends. Dennis, make up the fire and draw the curtains. Mr. Gerans, there is one corner of the hearth for you, and there is a corner also for Rose, and to her I entrust the bellows.'

Gerans winced at the reference to the bellows, and looked at Loveday. But he remembered that she could not have heard his father's remark, and his colour, which had flashed to his temples, disappeared again.

The little maid of twelve appeared, and laid the cloth, standing on tiptoe and stretching over the table to smooth out the creases. By the

time it was laid evenly, Loveday reappeared in
a cloth gown, and helped the child to arrange
the table. A pretty Derby tea service appeared,
inherited by Loveday from her mother, a rabbit
pie, cold, and preserves of whortleberry, and
blackberry, and strawberry, of her own making.
Then ensued a pause of a quarter of an hour,
during which the little maid ran to the nearest
farm for cream and butter.

Presently the tea-kettle came in, and was
given a final heating on the hall fire, to insure
that the water was really on the boil when
poured upon the Chinese leaves. The curtains
were drawn, the candles lighted, a faggot of dry
wood thrown on the fire, and the little party
drew to the table.

Then Rose uttered an exclamation of delight.
On her plate lay a little bunch of purple violets.
'Oh, Loveday! how sweet the flowers are! and
how sweet of you to give me them!'

'Our violets bloom here all the year round,
the glen is so warm and looe' (sheltered).

'Like the pretty thoughts and fragrant vir-
tues of your dear heart,' said Rose, eagerly.
'Of all flowers I love the violet best.'

'The violets of Nantsillan will not compare

with the rose of Towan,' said Dennis Penhalligan.

Rose tossed her head impatiently. 'Spare
me your formal compliments,' she said; 'mine
was a pretty speech that sprang spontaneous
from my heart, and yours is laboured and arti-
ficial.'

Rose was, at first, less exuberant in her
spirits than usual. What Loveday had said to
her in the parlour affected her, but only for a
while. She was too buoyant to be long depressed, and by the time tea was over she had
regained complete elasticity.

Dennis shook off some of his gloom, and endeavoured to be cheerful. He was very pleased
to have Rose at his table, yet at the same time
he was ashamed of the bareness of his room, its
white walls, its common furniture. He could
never dispel the sense of his poverty. He was
proud, perhaps vain, not of his appearance, but
of his abilities, and the sense of his being un-
worthily placed and hardly treated never left
him. He was ashamed of his table because the
cloth was coarse, of the forks because they were
of steel with black handles, of the preserves because they were of ordinary wild fruit. His

heart was so cankered with discontent that he could not see and rejoice over the comforts and cleanliness that were his, provided by the care of his sister. He never saw what advantages he had, but he was keen-sighted towards the deficiencies. There is no more dangerous mood than one that is dissatisfied, none more tormenting than that which is unthankful. Loveday had a daily struggle with him to bring him to a better mind, but was unsuccessful.

'Dennis,' she said to him, 'the world is a mirror which reflects our humours—laugh to it, and it laughs back to you; scowl at it, and it returns your defiance. It will answer you as you address it, like an echo, just a note lower.'

Dennis asked Rose during tea if she were fond of music.

'Music!' she answered, clapping her hands. 'Oh, I love it! I love nothing better.'

His dark face lightened as she said this. They had a passion in common.

'Then,' said he, 'I will play you a sonata of Beethoven's; that in C minor. It is my favourite; of others, I have to ask what they mean, but this one tells its own tale. I can play this better than another, not because I have practised it oftener, but because I can speak it through my fingers. Every note expresses a thought of my heart. As I interpret this sonata, it is the utterance of titanic defiance by one wounded in spirit; like a tamed eagle that longs to soar, but cannot, it beats its wings in frenzy and scorn, and gnaws its own heart out, because condemned to lie on earth when its proper sphere is above the clouds. It feels itself cast down and banned by a dark and inexorable power above which denies it light and air. In the *maestoso* you hear the agony of the soul; in the *allegro*, its defiance. There is a battle in which the restive spirit submits, and then revolts, cries out in fury against the iron fate which holds it down, and then throws itself sullenly with face to earth, in sob and moan. Here and there bright and melodious passages flash, like summer lightning, or pass as fragrant airs, but they do not lessen the darkness nor alleviate the pain.'

'Do you mean to tell me, Mr. Penhalligan, that all this is contained in a few pages of music?'

'You shall judge for yourself. You have heard my " Argument," now listen to the canto.'

He seated himself at the piano, and began to play. In a moment his soul was caught by the music, and he was carried away from his surroundings, as Elijah was caught and borne upwards in the chariot of fire. After a while, as he was playing, as perhaps he had never played before, his nerves excited by the presence of Rose, he became dimly conscious of something indistinct and irritating, a something that drew him down from his heights, and brought him into the vulgar presence of unworthy surroundings. By degrees he became aware what it was that marred his pleasure—it was a conversation carried on in a low tone in the room. He thought at first that the tiresome little maid was clearing away the tea things, and asking her mistress instructions; but when he paused to turn a leaf he heard Rose asking Gerans, ' But, really, cousin, what *is* a goose fair ? '

He tried to play on, but his interest in the music was gone. Loveday had watched his face, had seen his emotions throughout the performance quiver in his face, and now she read in it disappointment and anger. She went close to his side and said, ' Dennis, this is *caviar* to her ; play something lighter, the dance music in Lord Westmoreland's "Bajazet."'

Without answering, he allowed his fingers rapidly to glide into the frivolous, worthless music of the noble *dilettante*.

The talking ceased at once, and Rose's little feet beat the dance time on the slate floor.

Presently Dennis ceased. Then Rose clapped her hands. 'Thank you so much, Mr. Penhalligan. I have enjoyed myself greatly. But really, I did not think Beethoven could have written anything as fine. All the first part struck me as poor stuff, but the *scherzo* at the end was delicious.'

'Come round the fire,' said Loveday, quickly, stepping between her brother and Rose, to hide from her the expression of distress and disgust that passed over his face. 'I have got a lapful of chestnuts from our own tree. We must toast them in the embers ; and little Ruth will bring in glasses. You must taste my metheglin brewed from our own hives, and spicy with thyme from Towan Down.'

'Penhalligan,' said Gerans, 'are you going to the Goose Fair at Wadebridge?'

Dennis shook his head. 'Why should I go?'

'Loveday might like to be there, and eat Michaelmas goose.'

'Loveday is quite content to be at home,' said Miss Penhalligan.

'You must come, Dennis, and you also, Miss Penhalligan. The Goose Fair is an institution. My father goes, of course. We pick up my aunt and uncle Loveys on the way. It is settled that Rose is to go. I insist on your being my guests. Do not refuse me. Let me count— that makes seven. It takes four to a goose. We will have two. I dare say Anthony Loveys will come with his father and mother to make the eighth.'

Penhalligan looked at his sister doubtfully. Gerans went on: 'A moonlight night to drive home in over the moors. The Squire and the Loveyses can go in the chaise, and you and I, Dennis, and the young ladies in the gigs. There are our trap and yours available. If you will drive Loveday, I will drive Rose.'

'I shall not be able to go, I fear,' said Penhalligan, with darkening brow and quivering lip.

'Cousin Gerans,' exclaimed Rose, 'I should

have supposed that it lay with the ladies to choose their partners.'

' By all means,' answered Gerans; ' express your wishes, and they shall be obeyed.'

' Then I think you shall drive Loveday one way, and me the other way. I shall have the pleasure of listening to Mr. Penhalligan's compliments on one of the journeys, and to endure your uncouthness on the other. Which it is to be must be decided by lot. Here, Mr. Gerans, are my hands. One contains a violet, and the other nothing. Choose which you will have for the drive to Wadebridge. If you pick the violet you have Loveday, if you choose the other hand you elect simply me.'

' I take your left,' said Gerans. She opened her hand and showed the rosy palm.

' There, Mr. Penhalligan, yours is the honour and pleasure of driving me home by moonlight over the downs to Towan, after the Goose Fair. Will not that induce you to sacrifice your patients for a day?'

CHAPTER XIV.

THE GOOSE FAIR.

THE Goose Fair in the West of England is not a fair at which geese are sold, but is one at which geese are eaten. It takes place about Michaelmas—Old Michaelmas—and then all the country round the town at which it is held makes holiday. The labourers cast aside their flails and picks, put on their best clothes; the serving-maids beg a holiday with glowing cheeks and tears of entreaty; the farmers and their wives, and sons and daughters, and, till not many years ago, the gentry and the parsons, rode or drove to the market town with eagerness to eat goose. Geese ran over the commons in every village, and drank out of the ponds in every farm, and everywhere were eaten at home; nevertheless, a home-fed, home-roasted, home served-up goose was by universal consent a base and insipid dish when compared with Old Michaelmas goose ate in common in the market-town on Goose Fair Day. Better eat no mince pies at Christmas than omit to eat roast goose at Old Michaelmas Fair. Goose eaten then meant plenty throughout the ensuing twelvemonth. . The way in which this is expressed in the West Country vernacular is more precise than elegant. To write it would make the page blush the colour of the 'Globe.' Suffice it to say that he who eats roast goose on Goose Fair Day is sure not to have an empty stomach till next Michaelmas.

The Squire was a great stickler for old customs. Every year he drove to Wadebridge and picked up his married sister Barbara, and her husband Anthony Loveys, on the way, and carried them with him to the ' Lion's Head ' at Wadebridge, where they dined together—of course—on goose! When his own sons were old enough, and when young Anthony Loveys, his nephew, was of sufficient age to dine abroad, they were included in the party. Mr. and Mrs. Gaverock and Mr. and Mrs. Loveys sat down to one goose at a table by themselves; and Gerans, Constantine, and Anthony, junior, sat down to a second goose at another table by themselves ; and being young, hearty, and hungry, the three managed to demolish a goose between them, though, according to orthodox custom, it takes four to eat a goose.

On the fair day a smoke redolent of goose hung over the little town of Wadebridge. The atmosphere in every house was impregnated with it from cellar to attic. The inn kitchens were unable to cook all the birds required, and all the house kitchens in proximity to each inn lent themselves to be utilised for the occasion. The inns had not sitting-rooms to contain the guests, and beds were pulled to pieces and stacked in the garrets, and washstands piled one on another, that sleeping apartments might for the nonce be converted into eating-rooms. The gardens around Wadebridge had their sage reaped down, and their onions torn up and wheelbarrowed into the town days before, to stuff the geese that were to stuff the eaters at the fair. Feathers which had been a shilling a pound all the rest of the year dropped, as suddenly as the mercury before a cyclone, to ninepence. Children turned up their noses at butter, and enriched their bread with yellow goose fat. Dogs, cats, despised mutton and beef bones through the whole month of October, they were given such a surfeit of goose intestines.

To insure that every goose was well done, it was boiled the day before, and then roasted on the day of the fair; and goose broth—the water in which the geese had been boiled—was to be had for the asking by all the beggars, and poor, and sick in and round Wadebridge, but was despised and scouted by them, and so poured away for the pigs by those who kept pigs, and down the gutters by those who had none.

When the fair was over and the town re-lapsed into its normal stillness, and the smoke of the fires and the fumes of the roast lifted and were wafted away, then the Wadebridgians settled down to pies of gizzard and feet, and hashes of neck and doctor's nose which lasted a week, and soup of giblet and relics of stuffing becoming weaker and less savoury day after day.

The reader may suppose that we are about to describe to him the dinners themselves on Old Michaelmas Day, to revive in him the savoury recollections of many a sage-and-oniony and unctuous moment in his past : spots in life's pilgrimage on which it is a pleasure to look back, moments which were greasy but guileless. We are not going to do so.

At one table sat Squire Gaverock with his sister and brother-in-law and young Anthony; at the other the two young ladies with Gerans and Dennis. Old Gaverock carved his goose with experience, and helped himself to the flap of fat skin that covered the stuffing. Gerans squirted the gravy over the table, and in the faces of his companions, in his clumsy attempts to find the joints of the wings and legs. The old people had done their first helping before the young had begun their hacked and shapeless morsels. But time was made, like geese, to be killed. The afternoon was before them, in which, after a protracted, merry meal, to stroll about the town and look at the shows and shops.

Young Anthony Loveys was a tall, heavy young man, into whose constitution goose seemed to have largely entered. He spoke very little, ate hungrily, was blank in face, red complexioned, and puffy, with a rough skin. He could ride, and liked dogs; he drank readily with his father and uncle, but never became uproarious. By age he belonged to the younger party, but that party was not sorry to be without him at their table, when he would have contributed nothing to their entertainment.

To the goose succeeded apple tart with clotted cream; then cheese and celery, and a bottle of port. After that, the young people were at liberty to leave the table; but their elders, and the heavy Anthony junior, remained at theirs talking, arguing, eating apples, and drinking more wine. Mrs. Loveys, indeed, protested that she had shopping to do in the town, and during her absence a neighbour, also dining that day on goose at the 'Lion's Head,' took her place.

The morning had been bright and sunny, with a pleasant air from the sea. When the diners turned out into the street and square, they saw that a change in the weather had taken place. The wind had veered round to the north-east, had risen, and was bitterly cold. Heavy clouds were massed on the horizon and were rolling over and obscuring the sky. Some persons in the market-place said they had heard thunder; others said they had seen lightning, but had heard no thunder.

The delay in getting dinner, the insufficiency of waiters, and the general reluctance to break up from table, had brought the afternoon to half-past three before the inn was left for the sight-seeing and shopping. The fairing was done with shivers. The owners of stalls were with-drawing their wares under cover; darkness was settling prematurely over the town. Hark! A distant moan and then roar. In another minute down came snow in a blinding shower, whirled over Wadebridge and the valley of the Camel by a furious icy gale.

'Come here! Come in here!' exclaimed Dennis Penhalligan, drawing the ladies under a booth out of the snow and wind. The booth was a hut of rough boards.

There were various wares exposed on the counter of the booth where they stood, but the party did not regard them; they stood looking at the snow as it swept past.

The street was full of flying people, farmers and peasants who had come in for the day to enjoy the fair and eat goose, and buy at the stalls. Mothers had dolls, and little windmills, and wooden horses for their children, and as they ran they dropped some of these treasures. There rose much laughing and many shouts. The storm increased the merriment.

'Do look there!' exclaimed Rose; 'see that odd man!' She pointed to the figure of a pedlar who passed carrying a pack slung before him, a long basket covered with tarpaulin. The man was fantastically dressed, with a feather in his hair, and no cap on his head. He wore a long oilskin coat. As he passed the wind swirled the snow about him, so that he seemed to walk in the midst of an eddy of revolving flakes that half obscured him.

'How odd!' said Rose. 'Do you see the fellow, Gerans?'

'Yes,' answered the young man. 'But what amuses me most is that o'd farmer with the packet of lemon drops; the snow has melted the paper, and he is trailing the sweet things around him.'

'Now the man is gone,' said Rose.

'Come,' said Gerans, 'let us see whether there is anything in this stall that can attract us till the storm blows over.'

They turned and examined the wares.

They consisted of old iron; there was nothing they could buy.

'A pity we have not come where there were bonbons and cakes,' said Gerans. 'I would treat you to the whole contents.'

'At all events,' said Loveday, 'we have got shelter from the snow.'

Dennis was excited and irritable. The wine he had drunk had heated his brain without warming his heart. He was jealous of Gerans's attentions to Rose, which were marked, and he resented being behoven to his rival for the feast. He was angry with himself for having accepted the invitation, and he was angry with Gerans for having invited him. When he detected Gerans saying something to Rose which made her laugh, he suspected that the joke was about himself, his poverty, his want of professional success, his ill-humour. The dark veins in his brow swelled, and his lips quivered so that he was forced to bite them to disguise his agitation. He could not quarrel with Gerans over the cups for which the latter had paid, but he would be glad of an occasion for a quarrel elsewhere than at the table where Gerans was host. The observant eye of Loveday was on him. He felt it, and resented that also. He knew that she read his heart, and he was angry with her—his best friend—for doing so. He would have hidden his ill-humour, his envy, his hate, but he could not do so.

They turned to look again at the weather. As they did so, again the strange pedlar Rose had noticed came into sight, walking slowly against the storm. As he came up to the stall where the little party was clustered, he stood and turned and looked at them. His lips moved and he half opened his pack. They saw that he was deformed. He had not an ordinary hunch, but a something that protruded from the middle of his back in a strange peak. He was a singular-looking man, with long, ragged black hair. A band was tied round his head, holding his hair in place, and in this band were stuck a peacock's feather and a Cornish crystal. His features were bold, an aquiline nose, and arched, thick black brows. His complexion was coppery, his eyes were deep-sunken, and from the hollow sockets they gleamed with a mixture of appeal, provocation, insolence, and deference. He wore a glazed oilskin suit, very long which he kept wrapping and flapping

about him with his arms; beneath it the colour
of a red waistcoat or jacket, they could not
distinguish which, was visible when the water-
proof fell apart.   He wore long wading-boots.

He was followed by a white and liver-
coloured dog.   As he stood looking at the
little party an involuntary shiver ran through
them.

'I am cold,' said Rose.   'Let us move
away from here.   I do not mind the snow.'

'Let us go,' said Loveday to her brother.
'I have done all the fairing I care for.'

'That is, you have done none; for you
have not had money to spend.'

'I have bought what little I need,' said
Loveday, gently.   'After all, Dennis, we do
not want much, and what is the use of buying
what we can do without?'

The pedlar was gone.   A rush, blinding
and dense, of hail and snow mixed, went by,
and with his head down against it, followed by
his dog, went the man.

'Who is that queer man?' asked Rose.

'How can I tell?' answered Gerans.   'He
is quite a stranger—some showman or mounte-
bank.'

'His eye rested on me and made me feel colder than if I had been cut by a blast of east wind and snow.'

'Well, you will never see him again.'

'I wonder now,' said Rose, 'what he could have in that pack he carried before him. I have brought money in my pocket and have bought nothing.'

CHAPTER XV.

THE PEDLAR'S PACK.

'Halloo! You in here, Rose? Loveday? What! the lads and the maidens out in the storm?'

The voice was that of old Gaverock.

'You here too, Anthony?'

The voice was that of old Loveys.

'Come along, we have ordered coffee,' shouted old Gaverock. 'Here's myself and the rest of us old folks come to look for you through the snow.'

Hender stood outside the booth. At the same moment the pedlar was again seen, now standing beside him, and his dog ran round the Squire. Old Gaverock turned and looked at the dog, then he fixed his eyes with a wide stare on the pedlar. He put his hand to his brow, drew it over his eyes, which had in them a startled expression, and his mouth fell open.

'What is this? Who are you? What is here?' he asked. 'Come away, Rose; come away, Miss Penhalligan. Gerans, we must be driving home.'

'Oh, uncle!' said Rose Trewhella, 'who is that strange man? We have seen him pass several times. What has he got in that pack he carries in front of him? Do go and ask him, Gerans. You, Guardy!'

'Come away,' said old Gaverock, with a tone full of uneasiness. 'This is not fit weather for you girls. Come away; we must be returning home.'

He was manifestly ill at ease. He kept his eyes fixed on the pedlar with something like alarm in them. Rose, with her perversity of nature, now wanted to stay. A few minutes before she had wished to leave. But old Gaverock would take no refusal; he would allow of no delay. He drew the girls away from the booth towards the inn.

Gerans remained behind and went up to the pedlar, who had placed his pack on the snow at his feet.

'Have you any wares in your pack,' he asked, 'wares that would interest the ladies? You are a stranger here, are you not?'

'I have wares.'

'Let me look at them.'

'No; the ladies must see, not you.'

'Then bring the pack to the inn. They will be there some minutes before leaving Wadebridge.'

The pedlar, without more ado, stooped and took up the box of wicker-work covered with black oilcloth. As he was unable to carry his pack slung behind him, because of the hump in his back, he carried it in front, slung round his neck, as a hurdy-gurdy player carries his instrument.

'I will show my pretty things,' he said; 'they are not for you, sir, nor for any of the gentlemen—only for the ladies.' Then he followed Gerans to the inn.

The party was all there in the long room, well lighted and hot, waiting for the horses and traps to be brought round. When the pedlar appeared with his basket and raised the lid, every one crowded up to look in, expecting to find needles, thimbles, thread, and tape. But what was their surprise to find that it contained nothing but roses! Roses at that time of the

year—just now when hail and snow were driving
about the house, when the winter storm was
tearing every leaf off the trees and every
flower from its stem! It was true that the
blossoms were mostly those of monthly roses,
that bloom up till Christmas; still, the sight of
a basketful of them presented in a heated inn
parlour to men laden with wine and spirits, and
inclined to be uproarious, was incongruous.
The roses were done up in little bunches: the
pretty Bourbon, just introduced; the Noisette
and the China roses; buds with leaves, and
single flowers in full blow, with a little maiden-
hair fern.

The men laughed; some scoffed. The ladies
were delighted, and the young men eagerly
bought bouquets for them. Probably the pedlar
did a better trade in these perishable articles
than he could have done with needles and
threads.

'Guardy!' cried Rose, 'you must positively
take home a very large bunch for dear aunt.
You could bring her no fairing that would please
her better.'

'My love,' said Mr. Loveys to his wife,
' choose your posy and command my purse.'

'I must give one to you, Miss Rose, and another to you, Miss Loveday,' said Gerans.

'It is carrying coals to Newcastle to offer roses to the Queen Rose—the Sansparcille,' said Dennis.

'Really, Mr. Dennis,' exclaimed Rose, laughing, 'your laboured compliments overwhelm me!'

'You will allow me as well as Gerans to offer you a posy?' he asked.

'I have two hands,' answered Rose, gaily. 'I wish I had four, to carry a bunch in each.'

'Then pray choose.'

She thrust her hand into the basket, in among the flowers, and uttered a startled cry as she sharply withdrew it.

'What is the matter?' asked Loveday, standing up.

'Look! look!' exclaimed Rose. 'There is a toad among them, at the bottom, hidden by the flowers.'

'A toad! Impossible,' said Loveday, and put in her hand.

Rose grasped her wrist and drew her fingers away.

'Do not touch. I know there is; I felt it.

You cannot see—the rose leaves hide it—but I had a glimpse of the beast; it spits—poison.'

Dennis laughed sarcastically, and shook the basket. Then there emerged from under the sweet and delicate flowers, a little round, glossy, brown object.

Rose cried out, and shrank back Loveday recoiled also. Those crowding round the table shook it, and again the roses covered the object from their eyes. Whatever it was, it lay at the very bottom of the box.

'I know it is a toad!' said Rose, vehemently. 'I touched its cold and clammy body, and it sent a shudder up my arm and a chill to my heart. Look! there—again.'

The pressure of hands on the table, the thrusting of men against its side eager to see for themselves, gave movement to the box; and for an instant a round brown object appeared above the rose leaves and then dipped under them again.

'What have you got there?—in there, Hunchback?'

'Where?'

'There; under the roses, at the bottom of your pack.'

' Crushed roses, bruised rose leaves. Nothing else, gentlemen, that I am aware of.'

' But beneath the roses?' asked Gerans.

' Nothing at all.'

' There! See! Peeping up again above them.'

' This is the best way to ascertain,' said Dennis, and he turned the basket over on the table.

' My posies!—my flowers!—you will spoil them!' cried the pedlar in dismay.

The heap of flowers lay strewn about, and among the beautiful pink and white blossoms lay a small double-barrelled pistol, with rusty barrels, but with a polished curled handle of brown mottled wood; so shaped that at the first glance, as it peeped out from among the roses, in the uncertain light of the candles, it might readily be taken for a reptile. Dennis Penhalligan took up the pistol and examined it. As he did so a black spider emerged from the bore and ran over his hand.

The pedlar was uneasy, and wanted to have the weapon returned to him. He put out his hand across the table, with the oilskin sleeve on it, and tried to grasp the handle and take it

from Dennis, but the young man would not
give it up. He turned the pistol over, rubbed
the rust spots, and examined the lock; then
he handed it to Squire Gaverock, who was
clamouring to have a sight of the weapon.

'Pshaw!' exclaimed the old man. 'Do
you call this a pistol? It is more fitted for
ladies than men. It might knock over a sparrow,
nothing bigger.' He tossed the pistol back.
Another took it up and looked at it. So it
was passed round.

'What do you want for it?' asked Mr.
Loveys. 'It is worth the value of old iron,
nothing more.'

'It is not mine, sir; it is not for sale.
Give me my little pistol back. If I had thought
to sell it, I would never have put it among
flowers to rust.'

Dennis took hold of the weapon again.

'Pray mind what you are about,' said
Gerans. 'It may be loaded; and you are
pointing the barrel at me.'

'Will you sell it?' asked Penhalligan of
the pedlar.

'You do not want the ugly plaything,' said
his sister. 'What could you do with it?'

Play with it, as it is a plaything,' answered the young surgeon. 'Practise with it on a rainy day; that is pleasant sport for an idle hour. I will have the pistol. What is your price, Hunchback?'

'Price!' repeated the pedlar. 'It is not for sale; it is worth nothing. To set it to rights will cost money; but the stock is good. I will take a guinea for the thing.'

Dennis opened his purse, then coloured to the roots of his hair. He had not a guinea in his purse.

'Loveday,' he said in a low tone, 'lend me a few shillings.'

'My dear Dennis, I have nothing.'

'Do you wish very much to have the pistol?' asked Rose.

Before he could reply, an ostler came in to say that Squire Gaverock's carriage and the gigs were ready.

'The storm has abated,' said Mrs. Loveys.

'Oh, look!' exclaimed Loveday, glancing through the window, ' the moon is shining, and the street is white with snow.'

'Hail, hail!' corrected Gerans. ' The moors will be glistening white as we drive

home. I hope you have wraps, Miss Loveday ;
we shall meet the wind.'

In the bustle of preparation for the long
drive home the pedlar was forgotten. He took
the opportunity to refill his basket with the
scattered flowers.

'Are you ready, Miss Rose?' asked the
surgeon. 'My horse is impatient to be off.'

'Coming directly ; I have forgotten something.'

Gerans and Loveday started. The sky had
cleared—a few curdy clouds hung in it, like
ice-floes in a dark cold sea ; the ground everywhere was white and crackling under the feet
of men and horses.

The barouche with the Squire was shut,
but he shouted through the window for a drop
of cordial all round to keep out the cold.

'Now, Mr. Dennis, I am at your service,'
said Rose, coming out at the door; 'it is my
fate, I believe, to be driven by you. Fortunate !
for if you upset the trap, and dislocate my neck,
you are at hand to set it again.' He helped
her into his gig, and in another moment they
were driving homewards in the wake of Gerans.

. In a quarter of an hour they were out of

the valley, on the high road. On each side was moor, treeless, white, shining in the moonlight; rocks seemed like lumps of coal, bushes as fibrous tufts black as soot.

'Gerans is out of sight,' said Rose.

'He has a better horse than mine. One such as myself must put up with a cob.'

'Do you know, Mr. Penhalligan, I shall not go to another Goose Fair; one is sufficient in a life's experience.'

'Nor I,' said he.

'I do not think it is quite an entertainment for a lady. One generation becomes more particular than another, I believe. Our successors will be too nice to sit at table in an inn with men drinking, and go to a booth to do their shopping. I felt all the time that dear Loveday was out of place. But Mrs. Loveys liked it, and Mrs. Gaverock always attended.'

'When the ladies decline to attend the gentlemen will hold aloof. Then it will be left to farmers and their wives to frequent the ordinary.'

'I believe Gerans would not care to go unless accustomed to do so.'

'Gerans!' laughed the surgeon; 'he goes because his father says "Go"; and he eats his goose because his father puts the roast bird under his nose. If he obeys his wife, when he gets one, as he obeys his father, his daily meal will be off humble pie.'

'You are too hard on poor Cousin Gerans,' said Rose, in an injured tone.

'I am but repeating what *you* have said. You likened him to a dancing dog the other evening. I saw dancing poodles to-day at the fair, and remembered your simile.'

Rose said nothing, but moved uneasily in her seat. So they drove on, neither speaking.

The white moorland, cold and shining, was stretched to the horizon on both sides. The road was indicated only by granite stones stuck on end, capped with snow, casting black shadows away from the moon. Everything around was in white and black; there was no colour in the dark sky aloft, no colour in the inky sea, caught in glimpses between the headlands; no colour in the tortured thorn-bushes and rare crippled ashes come upon here and there. They might have been driving over the surface of the full moon.

Presently Rose said, 'Let us have done with joking on that subject. It has become distasteful to me.'

'Perhaps the subject of your jokes has been changed,' said Dennis, bitterly, 'and I am the unhappy victim of your raillery. I saw you laughing with Gerans.'

Rose opened her eyes wide. 'We were not thinking or speaking of you.'

'The unfortunate and the unhappy are not worthy to be thought of by those on whom fate smiles.'

'Why do you speak like this, Mr. Penhalligan?' asked Rose. 'You are not unfortunate, and have no right to be unhappy. You are very highly blessed in having a sister such as Loveday, and ought to be serenely happy in such a sweet home as Nautsillan.'

'I may have ambitions beyond a sister to keep house for me, and a hired cottage, scantily furnished, with slate floors.'

'You are young, and have the world before you,' said Rose, cheerfully.

'The world before me!' repeated Dennis with a sneer. 'A world like this'—he swept the horizon with his whip—'cold, dead, shelterless, over which to go, with head down against the numbing wind, without a gleam of sunshine to cheer, a continual winter, moonlight, and beyond '—he pointed with his whip to the black Atlantic—' the unfathomed sea of Infinite Night. It is now as it was of old in Egypt. Some are in day, whilst others are immersed in a darkness from which there is no escape.'

He put his hand into his overcoat pocket for his kerchief, as his brow was wet.

'What is this?' he asked in surprise, as he drew something from it. Insensibly he tightened the rein and checked the horse. In his hand he held a small pistol, and the moon glinted on its polished stock and rusty barrel.

Rose laughed.

'This is the pistol I saw among the flowers,' he said.

'Accept it as a little present from me,' said Rose, coaxingly but timidly. 'I saw you wished to have it, so stayed behind and bought it. Keep it for my sake.'

'And use it,' asked Dennis, 'should the necessity arise?'

CHAPTER XVI.

'PAS DE CHANCE.'

DENNIS was more than touched, he was deeply moved by the kindness of Rose. His blood rushed through his veins like lava streams. His hand shook as he held the reins.

'How good—how very good of you!' he said. 'I feel it the more because I am unused to receive kindnesses.'

He put the reins in her hand. 'You can drive for a minute whilst I look at your present. How I shall value it, words cannot tell; never, never will I part with it whilst I have life.'

He turned it over in the moonlight. The rust spots on it were like the marks—the blotches—on the back of a toad; the steel shone white in the moon's rays, flashed and became dark again. Dennis tried the cock.

'Don't span it,' said Rose; 'it may be loaded.'

Penhalligan laughed. 'Not likely. An old pistol, lying at the bottom of a basketful of roses. Loaded! Why should it be loaded?' He drew the trigger carelessly. At once a report followed, with a flash, and the bullet flew over the horse's head.

The beast, frightened at the discharge, bounded, kicked, and dashed forward. Before Dennis had time to wrest the reins from the hand of Rose, the horse had run the gig against one of the granite blocks by the roadside, and almost instantaneously the gig was over, and Dennis and Rose were in the road.

Penhalligan picked himself up. He was shaken, but not hurt.

Without a thought for his cob and trap, he ran to Rose, who lay on the snow motionless. In mad terror he picked her up, and spoke to her, but she made no answer.

'Rose! My dearest! Rose, for God's sake speak!'

He felt her arms, her feet; no bones were broken; the words she had said as he lifted her

into the gig recurred to him—but her neck was
not broken.

'Rose! Rose!' he cried, and clasped her
in his arms. He knelt on the hail- and snow-
covered ground and held her to his heart.
'My God!' he said, 'has it come to this, that
I have killed her I love best in the world?'
He turned her face to the moonlight. How
lovely it was! In his agony and passion he
put his lips to her brow, her cheeks, her
mouth. 'I may never have another chance of
kissing her,' he said fiercely. As he held her
to his heart it was as though he held her before
a raging furnace, and that the heat it gave
forth must restore her. He leaned his cheek
to her mouth, to feel if she were breathing ;
he laid his hand on her heart to learn if it
were beating. Then he put his fingers through
his hair, and held his temples, which were
bursting with the boiling, beating pulses of fire,
and his eyes were lifted to the black sky, in
which swam the chill, dead moon. 'My God!'
he said in a voice that shook with passion,
'give her to me, and I will be good. I have
not prayed for many years. I ask this one
thing now. Give her to me!'

He felt her move in his arms.

'Dennis,' she said, 'what is it?   What are you saying?'

'I am praying.'

'For me?'

'Yes—yes—yes, for you.   Only for you.'

'What is the matter? Where am I? What has happened?'   She disengaged herself from his embracing arm and tried to stand.

'We have been upset.   You are hurt?'

She felt her head. 'No,' she said, 'not much.   I lost all sense.   Now I am right. What happened?   Where is the gig?   Did we fall out?'

Now he looked round.

'The gig is broken.   There is my poor horse, fast by the head.   The rein has caught in the axle, and the axle turning has brought his head up to the wheel.'

'Can we not go on?'

Penhalligan shook his head.

'But what is to be done?   We cannot spend the night on the moor and sleep in the snow.'

'The chaise is coming on with Mr. Gaverock and the Loveys' party.   The young cub can turn out on the box, and you will travel home, inside.'

' But you ? '

Dennis shrugged his shoulders. ' What happens to me is of little moment. I must release my cob and ride him home.'

' I am so sorry. It is all my fault.'

' I regret the accident for one thing only.'

' What is that ? '

' It deprives me of your company for the rest of the way.'

' That is nothing.'

' To me—everything.'

' Even the cutting wind and the snow cannot freeze compliments from your tongue.'

Dennis led her to a block of granite and seated her upon it. He collected the wraps and folded them round her; if she would have suffered him he would have taken off his overcoat and laid it in the snow for her feet to rest in, and folded it over them to keep them warm.

' Mr. Penhalligan, I cannot, I will not permit this; you are over-kind to me and over-cruel to yourself. See the poor horse. Do release him, and tell me the true condition of the gig.'

'The horse must wait until you are taken away from me by the chaise. Every moment now is to me most precious.'

'Really, Mr. Penhalligan, you turn me dizzy again. Do attend to the horse.'

'The carriage may be here at any moment.'

'Well—the sooner the better for me.'

'But not for me, Rose! no, not for me!' He stood before her in the white road, with his right hand on his brow; the moonlight was full on his face; she could see it working convulsively, as the face of a man might work who was on the rack. 'Rose! dear Rose! I have held you for one moment in my arms, to my heart. I confess all. I touched your lips with mine, and have drunk from them madness! I know what I am, a man with no fortune, and no luck, a disappointed, an unhappy man. And you are born to enjoy life, without a care or a sorrow, or occasion for thought. I look at you as Dives in torment gazed at Lazarus afar off, and feel but too cruelly that there is a gulf between; but it is a gulf which love can overleap. Dives!' he laughed, and his laugh was shrill and startling in the night. 'I liken myself to Dives. The time for Dives to be cast

into hell and Lazarus to be translated to heaven
is over. Dives now mounts to Paradise, and
the poor and the sick and the aching in heart
and bone, and the sore of skin and racked of
brain, toss and ache and moan in life and in
eternity.' He spoke so fast, and in such a
passion, his breath coming in gasps breaking
his speech, that Rose could hardly catch what
he said. She was frightened at his vehemence,
and she put out her hand to lay it on his arm
and pacify him. He mistook her meaning, and
caught her hand in his.

'Rose! dear, dear Rose!' he cried, 'is it
true that my long night is turning to day?
That happiness is coming to me, even to me?
Oh, Rose! you have never known or dreamed
of love such as mine. I am not a poor, sleepy,
cold-blooded creature such as Gerans. I love
you. I have knelt here in the snow and stretched
my hands to God and asked for you. I who
never pray, I cannot endure life without you.
Rose, speak to me. Tell me you hear what I
say. Tell me that I am not to despair.' He
clenched her hand so tightly in his that she
cried out with pain. 'I have hurt you!' he
said; 'that is the nature of my love. I hurt

those I love.' He became cooler, and folded his arms.

Then the horse, driven desperate by the restraint of its head, began to kick furiously at the broken gig behind it.

'Do, Mr. Penhalligan—do look to the poor horse. Give me a minute to collect myself.'

He stood doubting whether to obey or not; then he saw, coming along the road from Camelford, two orange balls of light. The barouche was approaching.

'No,' he said firmly. 'I will have my answer now. It must be now. I must know whether I shall have you or lose you. On this moment everything hinges. I had not thought to speak, but the necessity drove me. I could not do other. Answer me.'

'Mr. Penhalligan,' began Rose, after a pause, with her eyes along the road, watching the approaching carriage lamps, and measuring the distance between them and the place where she sat, 'Mr. Penhalligan——'

'When you woke from your unconsciousness you called me Dennis,' he interrupted.

'Did I? That was because I was unconscious still—of what was fitting.'

'Answer me, Rose. There is but a moment more.' He also looked round. The tramp of the horses in the snow and hail was audible.

'*You are too late,*' she said slowly, articulating each word with distinctness. 'Gerans asked me on my way to the Goose Fair, and I said Yes.'

Then he burst into a wild, fierce, ringing laugh, and clasped his hands over his head, and wrung them there.

'Pas de chance!' he cried—'Pas de chance! It is always so.'

'Halloa! who are there?' was shouted in their ears. The barouche was level with him; the driver had drawn up.

Rose ran to the door and knocked. Old Gaverock and Mr. Loveys were out directly.

'It was my doing, all my fault,' said Rose, half crying, half laughing, and nigh on hysterics. 'I would drive, and, having the reins, upset the gig.' She turned to the surgeon. 'Mr. Dennis, whatever you may say to the contrary, I alone am responsible. It was my fault solely.'

'Curse it!' exclaimed old Gaverock. 'Who cares whose fault it was? The gig is broken and will have to be mended. You, Missie, will come home with us now. Penhalligan, how will you manage?'

'I shall ride home.'

'Here!' shouted the Squire, 'give me the light.'

He took the carriage lamp and looked about in the snow. 'Is there anything lost? What is this? Here is a pistol! Golly! very like that we saw to-day in the pedlar's pack.'

'It is mine,' said Dennis, and he took it from the Squire's hand.

Just then a large white owl flew hooting to and fro over the carriage and the little group, flitting like a great ghost-moth or swaying like a pendulum. At the same time, from under the carriage ran the white spotted mongrel of the pedlar, and began to limp on three legs round the party, then to throw itself on its back as one dead, then to leap with all fours straight up into the air and dance on its hind legs.

'How comes this brute here?' asked Mr. Loveys. 'What is it? Performing these antics here! To whom does it belong?'

Mr. Gaverock took the coachman's whip and lashed at the dog, hit it, and the beast began to howl, then dashed under the carriage, and disappeared.

The moon passed behind a white curdy cloud, and formed in it a ghastly ring of tawny hue ; it was like a single great owl's eye staring down at them from its socket of radiating feathers.

Young Anthony, useful when anything touching horses had to be done, had gone with the coachman to Dennis's gig, and disengaged the cob, with much shouting to the frightened beast. The brute was hot and trembling, his rough coat standing out, matted with sweat, and the steam rose from him. Anthony, junior, patted his neck and uttered ' Wohs !' in his ear, which produced a soothing effect, whilst the coachman extricated the gig from the place where it was wedged.

' Her ain't so bad used but what her may be made to run,' said the driver, speaking of the gig. ' The splashboard be scatt (broken to pieces) and the axle be bent : but otherwise her's middling sound. But her must be drove slowly and with care.'

' Where are my flowers ? Has anyone seen my beautiful roses ? I must have my posies,' said Rose. 'Oh, Guardy! let me have the lamp. I want them so much.'

'Never mind the roses,' said old Gaverock. 'We must get on our way.'

'But I do mind them,' answered Rose, 'not only for their own beautiful sakes, but also for the sake of those who gave them to me.'

Dennis approached. He said nothing, but held out the bunches. He had found them in the snow.

'Oh, thank you again, Mr. Penhalligan,' said Rose, looking at him and smiling, but somewhat timid still. 'There is no end to the favours you do me. You recover me out of the snow, and will not suffer my sweet namesakes to lie and perish in it.'

'Are all the cloaks and wraps in?' asked Gaverock. 'Come, Rose, we cannot spend the night here.'

'Yes, Guardy, I believe so. I am ready.'

'Then get in yourself.'

She stepped into the chaise; then, opening the window, put out her hand. 'Good-night, Mr. Dennis,' she said, in her prettiest tones. 'You have overwhelmed me with kindness. I shall never forget this night.'

' Drive on,' said Gaverock.

Then the yellow glare—the little of colour there was in that waste of white and black—moved forward, and Dennis Penhalligan was left in the road looking after the carriage. Though steeped in his own trouble, he started as he noticed a figure, which he thought was that of the pedlar, crouched behind the carriage, clinging to the great springs. In the moonlight he could not make out the nature of the coat, but his doubt ceased when he saw the shadow of the dog pursuing the barouche. The white dog with spots was itself scarce distinguishable against the snow and stony ground, but its shadow was black and defined. Dennis clasped his hands and moaned.

' Would to God we had both been dashed against these stone posts, and the life crushed out of us! Always too late for luck! The prize is out of my reach. Healing, rest, happiness, are for others, not for me. Pas de chance! Pas de chance!'

CHAPTER XVII.

THE FEATHERSTONES.

WHEN the hero of a novel falls overboard, is wrecked, or plunges off a cliff into the sea, unless he be produced within a few chapters with his nose eaten off by fish and his eyes pecked out by seagulls, the reader may be certain that he will turn up unhurt somewhere near the end of the book. Constantine Gaverock, it is true, is not our hero—indeed, we have no hero; but he is an important personage in our tale, and as we have not shown his bones in process of transformation into coral, nor his eyes into pearls, nor as undergoing any kind of sea-change, the reader may expect to see him again. Indeed, we gave the reader every reason to suppose that he would not be drowned, for we expressly stated that he was launched from the keel of the 'Mermaid' with two stone jars lashed about him, from which the spirits had been emptied,

and which were corked full of air.   Now, any
one with a particle of intelligence must know
that a man thus buoyed cannot sink.

Constantine did not sink.   On the contrary,
he floated like a bubble, and was driven by the
waves against the black cutter which old Gaverock supposed to be that of the rover Featherstone.   The men on board the vessel saved
him, but not before he had been beaten against
the side and was so stunned and bruised as to
be unconscious that he was in safety.

Constantine did not recover consciousness
till he was brought to land and had been in
bed for three days.   He did, indeed, occasionally open his eyes, when roused to take food,
but he closed them again, and dropped off into
sleep.   His head had struck the side of the
boat, and he was suffering from concussion of
the brain.   He dimly saw figures about his bed,
and was aware that he was in bed, but he felt
no interest to know who visited him, or where
he was, or why he was there.

On the third day, he woke from his stupor
and looked about him.   He was in a strange
room.   He raised himself on his elbow for
better inspection.   The room was large, with a

coved ceiling. There was a fireplace in which a fire of sea-coal was burning; in the corner was a spinet. The sun was shining in through the window, and he could see through the lat- ticed panes into a little court. Above the roof opposite were tree-tops, curled and leafless. He thought, on seeing this, 'I am somewhere near the coast.'

Whilst he was wondering and looking about him, the door opened, and a man of about thirty entered, very tall, grave, with dark hair and large hazel eyes; he was dressed in a dark suit, knee breeches and blue worsted stockings, like a farmer.

'I am glad to find you better,' he said in a quiet, precise tone. 'I supposed you would recover consciousness to day—if at all. The Lord be praised! I am glad, and I am thank- ful.'

'Not more than I,' said Constantine. 'But where the devil am I?'

'Hush!' said the man gravely. 'It is not through the agency of Satan that you are here; it is the Lord's doing, and it is marvellous in our eyes.'

'I should like to know where I am, and

how I came here,' said Constantine.   He spoke
with a raised tone, for he fancied that the man
was slightly deaf; he fancied it from the way
in which he turned the side of his head to him
when he spoke, and from the intent, earnest
expression of his face, as he listened to catch
what was said.

'You are at Marsland,' answered the man,
'you are our guest; our name is Featherstone
—Featherstone of Marsland.'   A slight colour
rose to his face, and a look of annoyance crossed
it.   'Unfortunately the name is known along
the coast.   If you come from these parts you
may have heard it—not spoken of with honour.
The fathers have eaten sour grapes and the
children's teeth are set on edge.   Of the Lord's
mercies, however, we are not utterly destroyed
for the iniquities of our parents; and perhaps,
in His pity, He suffers the children to expiate
by a blameless life, and by love and charity
and prayer, for the sins of former generations.'

Constantine turned red and white.   He was
in the house of a man whose father or uncle,
he knew not which, had been killed by his own
father.

'You were out in the terrible storm which,

I fear, sent many poor fellows to their last account,' Mr. Featherstone went on. ' Your boat and ours were close neighbours for some way; when yours capsized we picked you up. You were unconscious. But I must not speak to you more, newly restored. One thing only I ask. Put your hands together, as you cannot kneel, and consecrate to heaven your first returning thoughts.'

Then the grave man withdrew.

When he was gone, Constantine lay quiet, with his face to the wall, thinking. He was awkwardly situated. He had got into the house, of all others, he would least like to find himself in. Whereabouts he was he did not exactly know. Marsland was somewhere on the coast between Hartland and Padstow Point, he supposed, but he had never before heard the name. Whether it was in Cornwall or Devon he did not know. It certainly could be nowhere near his own home, or he would have heard of it. As for old Featherstone, whom his father had spiked, he was known all along the coast, and had his kitchens and cellars near every accessible bay, but he had never heard, that he remembered, where Featherstone's house was.

He had been as ubiquitous as the Flying Dutch-man.

Constantine could not think for long. His head was painful, and his thoughts began to wander when he tried to concentrate them.

Presently the door opened again, and a young lady entered, dressed in grave colours, but with a fresh and rosy face and pleasant, kindly expression. She had dark hair, and, what goes so charmingly with that, violet blue eyes. She had some needlework in her hands. She seated herself in the window and sewed. Constantine watched her. He thought her very pretty. There was a purity and innocence in her face which were more attractive than her beauty. Beautiful she properly was not, as her features were not regular, but her face was agreeable. The young man saw a likeness in her to the man, and concluded that she must be his sister, not his wife. His features were much more pronounced and regular than hers. He had a strongly characterised aquiline nose, dark eyebrows, and rather sunken eyes. She had not the same sort of nose, nor as heavy brows, yet there was an unmistakable family resemblance between them.

She saw that he was watching her, and looked round smiling.

'I am glad you are better,' she said, in a gentle voice with a Cornish intonation; 'we have been very anxious about you. We thought, if you did not rouse to-day, you would not rouse at all. And now, you must not talk, or trouble your poor head about anything you see or hear. Rest and be thankful. I am Juliot, Paul Featherstone's sister, and your nurse.'

'I am fond of music,' said Constantine. 'It would be the best medicine for me if you would play me something.' She threw down her needlework at once, and went to the spinet, opened it, and played 'All people that on earth do dwell.'

At the first notes, a rich deep bass voice rose from the court outside, singing the psalm, and Juliot's sweet, untaught, but musical voice sang also.

When the psalm was done, Constantine said, 'I thank you. Can you sing me something else? I should like something of Mozart.'

'I don't know anything of his, though I believe he wrote masses,' said Juliot. 'I play mostly sacred music. My brother does not care for any other. I can play you some of Tallis or Purcell.'

'Anything,' said Constantine; ' but it is not very lively; perhaps, however, it may be more soothing.'

'My brother Paul likes psalm tunes most of all,' she said, ' and so I play more psalm tunes than anything else. I can play and sing Jackson's "Te Deum" if you like, and "Angels ever bright and fair."'

'What sort of music do you like best, yourself?' asked Constantine.

'I!' exclaimed Juliot, modestly colouring— 'I—oh I—I do not know. I never considered. Of course I like that which pleases Paul best.'

'Does Mr. Featherstone object to your playing other than sacred music?'

'Oh no,' answered Juliot, frankly, turning her honest face, and looking full at him out of her honest violet eyes, ' not at all. Paul is not a Methodist. I can play gavottes and quad- rilles ; and he and I sing together Jackson's pretty duet, "Time has not thinned my flowing hair." But he says that no music speaks to his heart like the old psalm tunes. Whenever Paul is fretted about anything, or has met with annoyance, I can always bring his gentle, sweet look back on his dear face with a psalm tune. When I saw that you were awake and looking a little troubled, I played the " Old Hundredth." I thought it would have the same effect on you as it does on my brother.'

' Is he married ? ' asked Constantine.

' Paul married !' echoed Juliot, and laughed. ' I cannot fancy him with a wife. And yet she would be a happy woman who won him, for Paul is the gentlest of men. The animals all love him. When he goes out on the cliffs, the gulls come round him in flights ; and the sheep run to him when he appears on the common. As for the cows and horses—I am sure they adore him. I never hurt an animal, that I know, but they will not come to me as they go to Paul. The people round look on him as some one quite out of the ordinary, and come to him to have their arms and legs struck when suffering from swellings, and they bring him kerchiefs to bless, when any one has cut himself in the hay or corn-field, that he may stop the flow of blood.'

' But—does this succeed ? '

' Of course it does. Paul would not do it

else. But he is very humble, and it pains him if anyone says it is because he is so good. *I* think that is the reason. He thinks that it is given him that he may do a little good to make up for the great wrongs done to men, and the sins committed in the sight of God, by our uncle—Red Featherstone.'

'I do not know quite where I am. Am I in Devon, or Cornwall, or in Wales?'

'You are in Devon. This is the parish of Welcombe. Our little Marsland brook runs down to the sea and divides the counties and parish from Morwenstowe. We have a little harbour: it is the only bay in which in decent weather a boat may run in and be safe. We keep a boat there. Paul is very particular about his boat. It is the old cutter that our uncle had. When there is a storm, my brother is on the look-out to help distressed vessels, and save those who are in peril. Paul is so good. He was returning from Hayle, where he had some business, when he saved you, not so far out from Black Rock, where the people say the spirit of our poor uncle is engaged weaving ropes of sand. At one time we heard a great many stories about what went on in his time; of his wickednesses, of how he wrecked vessels, and murdered the crews when washed ashore, and of how he plundered on the coasts of France and Wales. But now we are told nothing; the people know that it distresses my brother to hear these tales. It is now a great many years since he was killed. If ever there was a case of murder, that was one— a man called Gaverock ran him through with an old spear whilst he sat in the sun on a rock warming himself. It was a treacherous and cruel act, though I admit my poor uncle deserved his death. People say he wilfully wrecked vessels, and if sailors and passengers swam ashore he killed them; but I cannot believe this; I think this an exaggeration. Do not talk to Paul about his uncle; he cannot endure it.'

Just then Paul Featherstone came in.

'You are not overstraining our patient's attention?' said he. 'Remember, he must be spared.'

'Paul, I have been telling him where he is—he did not quite understand.'

'You are in Marsland in Welcombe,' said

Mr. Featherstone, 'and you will also find a Welcome in Marsland.' He turned to his sister. 'I am making a joke, Juliot.'

'So I hear. You are very humorous, Paul.'

'Will you bring up the beef broth for our friend?' said Paul Featherstone; 'I believe it is quite ready.'

'I hope my sister has not made you talk more than your strength can bear?' said Mr. Featherstone, addressing Constantine.

'Not at all; she has been speaking to me, and playing and singing for my pleasure.'

'Juliot is always ready to do a kindness. Her heart overflows with goodness. In Welcombe, near the church, is a holy well to which people came in Catholic times for the blessed water that healed infirmities and cleared eyes of the scales that covered them. The parish takes its name from this well. It never fails. The limpid spring never diminishes, never runs dry, and all the way down to the sea, whither its waters run, the grass is green and flowers bloom. My sister Juliot's heart is a better holy well than that. It also never fails, and whithersoever its influence reaches it bears healing, strength, and beauty and love. I am glad you are here, to know Juliot. Do not raise your voice to speak to me. I can hear. I am not as deaf as you suppose.'

'I cannot sufficiently thank you for your kindness,' said Constantine.

'Oh, I do nothing. My sister thinks and cares for you. I am only her servant, and do what she designs. I am the hand that executes what her head and heart devise. I hope you will not think me wanting in courtesy if I ask your name.'

'Gaverock,' answered Constantine after a pause, and with some nervousness.

'Rock,' said Mr. Featherstone, who had not caught the full name. 'Now that is indeed curious, that the Rock should come to the Stone, whereas generally the stone comes from the rock. Our name,' he explained, 'is Feather-stone.'

Just then Juliot came in, bearing a bowl of soup on a tray.

'Sister,' said Paul, turning to her, 'our patient, whom by God's providence we have been able to help, is called Rock. Mr. Rock—

my sister, Miss Featherstone. Juliot, I have made a joke. I have said that now the rock has come to the stone instead of the stone proceeding from the rock. Do you follow me?'

'Oh, Paul, how clever, how humorous you are!'

CHAPTER XVIII.

MARSLAND.

MARSLAND HOUSE was built by William Atkyns in 1656, as a stone in the wall testifies. It is one of the most picturesque and delightful specimens of a small gentleman's house of the seventeenth century that we know. Not that it has architectural adornment. Of that it is absolutely free, but that it remains to this day perfectly untouched. It stands as it was when built, without an addition, and without a stone of the structure having been thrown down. An avenue leads to a little gatehouse that closes with strong oak doors. In this gatehouse lived the porter, with a peephole to command the avenue, and windows to light him, opening into the first court—quadrangle it is not, but an oblong court, before the face of the house. The entrance is from the east, and the face of the house is to the east, away from the sea.

The north side of this court is closed by a high wall. On the south side is the wall of the garden, with a door in it; the ground slopes rapidly to the south into the glen of the Marsland brook, and the garden takes all the sun, and is screened from the sea-gales by a dense wood of beech. The most prominent feature in the façade is the immense hall chimney forming a buttress, one side of which is utilised as the wall of the porch. The front consists of several gables of irregular height, charmingly picturesque. If we enter the porch, we pass through the house by a passage one side of which screens off the hall, and the other the kitchen and cellar and buttery. We then emerge upon the quadrangle of the mansion, into which the hall also looks, westward, and in which, on the north, are the drawing-room windows, securing by this arrangement shelter and sun. The west side is formed of sundry domestic buildings, and the south side is occupied by the servants' apartments.

Marsland Coombe is the most beautiful on this portion of the north Cornish and Devon coast. It is deep, clothed with oak coppice, and opens on a lovely bay. But scarcely a tourist who visits the coast thinks of looking in on this gem of old English country life and architecture. Since visitors have frequented this coast, settlers from the metropolis and elsewhere have come, and have built mansions—such miracles of hideousness that the traveller may rub his eyes, and, looking from the modern to the ancient, ask whether, after all, we have progressed during the two hundred years since Marsland was built. At the present day, Marsland, like so many other mansions of the gentry of a century or two ago, is turned into a farmhouse, and no guide-book calls the attention of the tourist to its beauty.

At all times Marsland was out of the way. The old north coast road from Bideford to Stratton, which is as ancient as British times, runs along the watershed of the streams which empty after a brief course down the thousand coombes into the sea, and, on the other hand, of the Tamar and Torridge. This watershed is a long backbone of elevated moorland within sight of the sea. Between it and the ocean are numerous—innumerable—deeply cleft valleys, becoming deeper as they near the sea, without the intervening hills becoming lower. The consequence is that a road skirting the cliffs would be a road consisting of scramble and slide up and down hills as steep as mediæval high-pitched roofs. Let the reader look at the back of his hand, and he may imagine a road taken across his knuckles to represent the high road, and his fingers with the clefts between will well represent the conformation of the land between that road and the sea. His finger-ends accordingly figure for precipitous headlands standing out of the ocean. The ravine between his index finger of the left hand and the middle finger represents the Welcombe valley, near the head of which stands the little parish church. The fissure between the middle finger and the ring finger symbolises the Marsland glen, which divides the counties. Halfway between the knuckle of the hand and the finger-nail, on the slope to the south, lies old Marsland House. The valley between the ring finger and the little finger is that of Morwenstowe, and the end of the ring finger is the splendid crag of Hennacliff, rising 450 feet sheer out of the waves. The high road traverses the bleak and barren moor, where the stiff clay soil refuses to yield anything but rushes and gorse, and this dreary country stretches away to the east, and in it rises the Tamar. On the other side the coombes are fertile, and, being sheltered by the folds of the hills, give pleasant pasture meadows and leafy coppices. To the present day there is no inn in either Welcombe or Morwenstowe, nothing to invite the traveller to diverge from the high road to visit these glens. At the time of which we write, some seventy years ago, this angle of coast was as little visited as Iceland, and those who dwelt in it were unknown beyond the moor side and road.

The Atkyns family, who, in the seventeenth century, owned the estate of Marsland, did not appear at the last heralds' visitation of Devon and Cornwall, in 1620, probably because they did not hear in their isolated nook that the heralds were holding inquisition as to who were gentle and entitled to bear arms and who were to be discounted as *ignobiles*. But though the Atkyns family did not then appear at Barnstaple on September 9, 1620, when the heralds held their court, there can be no question as to the antiquity and the gentility of the family.

But the Atkyns family went, as nine out of

every ten old families have gone; and at the time of which we are telling, and indeed for some hundred years before, Marsland had been in the hands of the Featherstones.

Should the tourist be induced by this account to diverge from the main road and visit Marsland, let him look in the side of the hedge of the lane descending into the coombe, and he will observe the entrance to one of Featherstone's kitchens, a vault, arched and walled with brick, filled in indeed, but still structurally uninjured and readily distinguishable. In it he hid his spoils; the place was easily accessible from the house, but the goods were not stored in his house, lest on a domiciliary visit they should be found by the constables.

When Constantine was left to himself, he considered what had taken place. He was not sorry that his name had been mistaken. He would make no attempt to correct the error into which Paul Featherstone had fallen. Why should he? It would do no good. It would only give annoyance. It might cause his expulsion from the house.

Constantine took the world as it went, very easily. He liked to be comfortable, and not to

have much to do. He was averse to the roughness of his father's ways, and he was not sorry
to be now away from home. Dennis Penhalligan had given him three days for communi-
cating the fact of his marriage to his father.
The time was now past, and no doubt the old
man knew by this time, if he were alive, the
secret that had been kept from him. Of his
father's safety he was not, however, sure, and
he resolved, without saying anything to his
hosts, as soon as he was able, on going to
Bude Haven and making inquiries.

Next day he was better and got up, but
could not leave the room. He was surprisingly
weak. He was amazed at himself, how his
strength had gone in a few days. His head
was still painful, especially when he exercised
it, so that he was glad to have cold compresses
applied. Juliot attended him, and was so kind,
and earnest in her desire to relieve his pain,
and to see him recovered, that he felt disposed
to make the most of his weakness and suffering.

During the ensuing days he sat up longer
than he had been able to do at first. He saw
a good deal of Paul Featherstone, who took
every opportunity of visiting him; but he saw

most of Juliot, who brought her work to his room, and sat with him the greater part of the afternoon.

'You will not see Paul to-day,' she said once. 'He is gone over to Stanbury, which belongs to us. It came through my mother, and Paul has to go there two or three times a week. It tires him, as he must ride : there is no driving on these by-roads, and Paul cannot ride well, it hurts him. He received a slight injury when he was young, which makes it painful for him to ride, and it is too far for him to walk with ease, our hills are so steep. My mother was a Stanbury, and she brought the estate to us.'

'Does that, then, belong to your brother as well as Marsland ? '

'It does and it does not. Properly it belongs to me, and Marsland is Paul's; but it does not matter—what is his is mine, and what is mine is his. There is no mine and thine between us.'

'But if he or you were to marry it could not go on like this.'

'I do not know. We have neither of us given a thought to that,' answered Juliot, blushing. 'It is so unlikely. We see nobody. We visit no one, and no one visits us. Paul cannot go far, as I have told you; he is not very strong, and it hurts him to ride. Besides, the ill-fame of our family through two or three generations has cast us into isolation. When Paul and I grew up we knew no one, and no visitors came to this house which bore so bad a name, and so we have lived to ourselves. We are very happy, and quite content, and want no change.'

'But would you not wish Paul to marry and give you a sister-in-law? You must need some lady friend to whom to open your heart.'

'If Paul were to marry—but the thought is so strange I cannot grasp it—I should love the wife he chose very dearly, for his sake, but I do not know that I want her. I keep no secrets from Paul, and Paul tells me everything that passes in his mind. I am sure you never, though you may have travelled very far, you never met with so beautiful and sincere a mind as that of Paul. He is so good. He is a little too trustful, if he has a fault; he believes that every one else is as good as himself.'

'But you will marry some day, and what about Stanbury then? And Paul, how would he like to have that cut off, after having managed it with Marsland so long?'

'Paul! Oh, Paul would always do what is right, and would not have a wish contrary to what he thought was right. Besides,' she said, going on with her needlework hastily, 'the thing will never be. It is not possible.'

'What is Stanbury worth?'

Juliot laughed, and looked round at him frankly, with her pretty, deep violet eyes—so pretty under their long dark lashes. 'I do not know. I have not an idea. I do not suppose my brother even could tell you. It is a nice little property, and the Stanburys lived on it for many generations. They were not great people, like the Grenvilles, and Rolles, and Arundells, but a very long way behind. I suppose the property is much the same as this in value, but no one knows less about these matters or cares less than myself.'

'Why does not your brother put in a farmer at Stanbury?'

'He either does not like to let it, or cannot. You see, Stanbury never has been a farm—I mean it never has been let. My mother's family lived there from generation to generation, and

Paul hardly likes to turn it into an ordinary farmhouse. Besides, I am not sure that he can let it on lease, lest I should marry—not that it is likely—in which case——' She did not finish the sentence, but got confused and red.

'I understand. Should you marry, you and your husband would go to Stanbury. I do not suppose Paul can let the place on lease.'

Nothing more was said for a few moments; Juliot sat with her needle in hand, looking out of the window, thinking. Presently she broke the silence with, 'I wish Paul had not to go there so much, it always over-tires him. He never complains, but his eyes become sunken in his face; then I know he is over-done, and has suffered. It does him good to be out of doors, and he has enough to occupy him here, in looking after Marsland Farm; but the journeys to Stanbury hurt him. I wish he would get some good, conscientious man to attend to the estate for him. He has had so much trouble with the caretakers he has put in. Some have turned out drunkards, others have been dishonest, and the last man has been in deep with the smugglers, and actually let them store away their run goods in the place. Paul was really angry about that. It takes a great deal to put him out, but that did annoy him, and no one about sympathised with his feelings, and thought he behaved very unjustly to the man, when he gave him notice of dismissal. As if Paul could be unjust!' She held up her head with a pretty pride. 'No one but I, his sister, know what it costs Paul to dismiss a man from his service. It costs him many wakeful nights. He turns the man's conduct over in his mind, and tries to find excuses for him, and he is over-ingenious in doing so. But even when he finds these excuses, he still knows when he must give dismissal, for he has to consider the example to others. I believe it gives him a heartache more than the man he turns away. I hear him sighing, when he is not conscious that any one is near; and, indeed, he sighs involuntarily, without knowing it, when I am present, and is reproaching himself for undue severity. I think a conscience may be over-tender.'

'I quite agree with you,' said Constantine. 'The hedgehog is sensible, it does not coil itself up with the prickles inwards. Now, shall we have some music?'

She put down her needlework instantly and went to the spinet.

'Do I hear Mr. Featherstone reading aloud in the evening?'

'Yes. He is fond of books, but we have not many. He is reading now Mr. Brooke's "Fool of Quality." Do you know it? My brother is very fond of the book. It is in six volumes. Sometimes he reads poetry, Crashaw and Vaughan, and George Herbert. If it would give you pleasure, he would come up here and read, and I would come also. He was afraid to offer it, lest it should be too much for your poor head. My brother wishes to do all in his power to make you happy and comfortable, and —the "Fool of Quality" is a mighty pleasant book. On holidays he reads Nelson's "Fasts and Festivals."'

CHAPTER XIX.

STANBURY.

WHEN Constantine was thought sufficiently con-
valescent to come downstairs, Mr. Featherstone
went to him in the morning, and laid some
garments on a chair by the bed.

'Mr. Rock,' he said, 'you have conferred
on my sister and me real favours as well as
affording us great pleasure. You will not, I
trust, shrink from extending your kindness
to us.'

'I—what have I done?' asked Constantine,
sitting up in bed. 'It is I who am the recipient,
not the conferrer, of favours.'

'Mr. Rock,' said Paul Featherstone, 'to
house the shipwrecked, to nurse the sick, to
minister to those who need a helping hand
through poverty, or weakness, or accident, is to
my good sister and, secondarily, to me such a
blessed privilege, that we cannot be satisfied till

we have added to our pleasure that of clothing those who are deprived by disaster of their customary wardrobe. Whilst you have been confined to your bed, we have taken the liberty of calling in a village tailor, and he has fashioned you a suit out of some claret-coloured cloth I happened to have in the house. He had your suit in which you were wrecked as his pattern, and I believe you will find it a decent fit, though mayhap the colour of the stuff be not to your liking. As to your linen, Juliot has cared for that. You have seen her busy with her needle; she has supplied you with what is necessary. Do not thank me,' said Paul Featherstone, holding up his hand, as he noticed that Constantine was about to speak ; ' it is we who have cause to thank a loving Providence which has put the opportunity into our hands. We live so quiet a life here, and see nothing of the world, that a visitor sent us is a friend given us, and, having few friends, it is a delight to us to help as best we can those whom God bestows on us.'

He bowed with old-fashioned courtesy and left the room. Constantine got up and dressed. The suit, though made by a village tailor, was well made ; it was after the cut of his garments got in Exeter. He stood before a glass and looked at himself in them. He was pleased with his appearance. He made a fine figure of a man. His illness gave a look of refinement to his face. He was a good-looking young fellow, and he was never more conscious of this than at the present moment. He put his hand into his pockets, and found in one a folded and sealed paper, addressed to himself, on opening which three bank-notes fell out, one for ten pounds and two for five. A present from Paul Featherstone, or a loan, according to Constantine's circumstances. Not a word accompanied the notes. If Constantine had means, he would repay the advance ; if he had not, Paul would never ask for the money—he was free to keep it.

'What nice, simple people these are !' said young Gaverock. 'They understand what a person wants, without forcing him to ask. This is what I consider good manners. I had to plague my father with my necessities before I got anything out of *him*.'

The moment Constantine's foot was heard on the landing, Paul and Juliot ran to his assistance. The staircase was steep, and they thought he might need support in descending. Therefore, each gave him an arm, and he went down with his right hand resting on the arm of the sister and the left on that of the brother.

He noticed that both were flushed when they conducted him into the little low-ceiled hall. They were flushed with pleasure at getting their guest downstairs, and seeing him so much improved in health. They were like children, pleased with small matters, and pleased that others should be happy and well.

By the hearth was an armchair, and they led him to it; and when he was seated, Paul clasped his hand and wrung it, and said, 'I shall always remember this day. I am so glad —so glad!'

Tears came up into the deep violet eyes of Juliot, tears of sympathy and pleasure. She said nothing, but Constantine saw that her heart was with her brother's, full of happiness, because he was sufficiently recovered to come downstairs.

'Juliot,' said Paul, with a smile, 'we have now a *vested* interest in Mr. Rock.'

'Yes, quite.'

'That was a joke, Juliot.'

'You quite sparkle, Paul. You are so witty.'

'I am sorry to have to leave you, Mr. Rock, on such a joyful occasion,' said Mr. Featherstone, 'but I am obliged to go over to Stanbury. Perhaps, when you are well enough, in a week or two, you will accompany me. I have some annoyance there.'

'If I can be of any service to you, here or there, now or at any time, command me,' said Constantine ; 'I am not ignorant of law.'

Paul shook his head. 'We have nothing to do with law here. I would rather suffer the extremity of injury than prosecute any one.'

'And I have had much experience in farm management.'

'That is another matter,' said Mr. Featherstone ; 'and, indeed, therein you may do me great service. But of that we can talk at another time. I again apologise.' He bowed himself out. 'Juliot,' he said, in the door, 'you will entertain Mr. Rock in my absence, that the time hang not heavy on his hands.'

Constantine looked about the little hall with some curiosity. It was very plain, with a slated floor ; a little dull, as both windows looked into yards enclosed by high walls, east and west, and the sun was not shining into either. Indeed, the sun that day was not shining at all. A long oak table occupied the centre with peg holes at the end, showing that in former times it had served not only as a table at which to eat, but also as a shuffle-board on which to gamble. Over the mantel-piece was a picture, apparently a portrait, badly painted, in a black frame. It represented a man, at full length, but the size of the picture was small. Constantine looked at the painting and was struck by it. The man was represented in a red waistcoat and black velvet coat, and he had a white spotted dog at his side. He wore high boots, but instead of a cap had a strap round his head confining his thick black hair, and in the strap was stuck a peacock's feather, where the band was fastened by a sort of brooch with a white stone in it, probably a Cornish crystal. The features were pronounced—an eagle nose, and arched brows, with the eyes sunken under them. The mouth was hard and the jowl heavy.

Juliot noticed that Constantine's eyes were on the picture, and that it excited his interest.

' That,' she said, ' is the likeness of our uncle,

the wicked Featherstone, who was killed by a man called Gaverock. He was so wicked that the parson would not bury him in consecrated ground and read the service over him ; so he is laid just outside the wall. Paul thinks, and of course he is right, that the shadow of his evil influence hangs over the place and the family. He quotes Scripture to prove it ; but I am sure of one thing, there is none of the sinful nature of our uncle in dear brother Paul, who is as good a man as old Featherstone the Rover was bad.'

'What a curious fashion for a head-dress ! ' said Constantine.

' Whether he wore that or not I cannot say. I dare be bound there are people in the place who could tell ; but Paul does not speak about the old Rover, nor does he wish me to converse with them about him. The subject is painful to Paul. He feels it very much. I have thought—but I may be wrong—that the plume and the crystal may be a fancy of the painter to express the name, Feather-stone.'

'I see that your brother is like his uncle, except about the chin and mouth. He has the same nose, and eyes, and brow.'

'But nothing—nothing whatever in character.'

'Was that your uncle's spotted dog?'

'That—yes. The dog lay down on his grave, and never left it, would eat nothing, and died. So there must have been some goodness and kindness in the old Rover, or the dog would not have attached itself to him. When the dog died, it was buried beside its master— that is, a hole was made in the earth by his grave, and the brute was laid there.'

About a week after this, Paul Featherstone said to Constantine, 'Do you not think that a ride would be beneficial to your health, Mr. Rock? You are heartily welcome to the use of my cob, as much and as often as pleases you.'

'Thank you,' answered Constantine; 'I should like a ride greatly. If I can be of service to you at Stanbury, to take a message, or to see whether an order has been executed, command me.'

'Certainly,' said Paul; 'you can oblige me greatly. The roofs were badly used by the gale, and I sent a wagon for slates. The masons are there, and should have reslated where the roofs were ripped. The water has been kept out for the time with hurdles and straw.'

'I will go there to-day.'

'And,' continued Paul, 'you may inquire of old Carwithen if he has got work. He has acted as hind for me hitherto—that is, for my sister—Stanbury belongs to her—and I have had to dismiss him, but I allow him to remain till he finds a suitable situation. The old man has abused my confidence. I am sorry. I liked him. Ascertain for me whether he has heard of a place, and I will thank you.'

Constantine enjoyed his ride. The air was mild, the sun shone, and the sea sparkled. Lundy Isle was full in view, its granite cliffs white in the sunshine. The leafy copse-covered coombe basked in the last warm light of declining autumn. The leaves were russet as the bosom of a redbreast. On the high land the gorse still bloomed; its golden flowers were, however, sparse. In the hedgerows the long glossy hart's-tongue ferns were unshrivelled by frost.

'I like this country,' said Constantine, looking round. 'It is more homelike than Towan.

I could be very comfortable here. It is not quite so bleak as about Padstow, and the people don't seem so rugged as my father and his set.'

He passed Morwenstowe valley and church, and ascended the hill opposite. He inquired his way, and was directed to Stanbury. 'Bless my soul!' said Constantine, 'what an out-of-the-world corner one is in here! Why, one might spend a life here unknown to the rest of the world, and without hearing how the rest of the world fares. That is just the sort of life I should like.'

He arrived at last at the house : it was small and comfortable and unpretentious. The land about it seemed good. 'One might fare worse than on this estate,' said Constantine. Then, as a man approached, he asked, 'Are you Richard Carwithen ?' The man was rough and old, very broad-shouldered, with haybands tied about his legs, below the knees. 'Ay,' answered he, 'at your service, Richard Carwithen ; and you, sir, I reckon, be Mr. Rock, as we've heard of at Marsland. Will you come in and have a drop of something to keep the cold out ? '

'Take the horse, please, and I will go round with you. The master has asked me to see if the repairs are done.'

'The master!' repeated Carwithen. 'Stanbury don't belong by rights to he! Stanbury belongs to the lady, and he who takes the lady takes Stanbury. More's the fool he who don't seize his chance while he may.' He looked at Constantine and laughed. Gaverock coloured to the roots of his hair.

'Has the gale done you much harm here?' asked he.

'Ripped off slates here and there, as a gale be like to,' answered Carwithen. 'Providence, that cares for sparrows, cares for slaters and shipwrights, and makes work for both; it tears the roofs away and sinks vessels with the same blast.'

'Were there many wrecks on the coast, that you have heard, in the last gale?' asked Constantine.

Carwithen shrugged his shoulders. 'Naught to signify,' he said. 'There was a boat washed ashore at Bude, the "Mermaid."'

'All hands lost?'

'The skipper came ashore all right.'

'Any more?'

'A schooner went to pieces in Widmouth —her name was the "Marianne"—just off Featherstone's Rock. I reckon that was the vessel in which you were. Bound for Bristol. All hands lost but you. That was the boat you was in, warn't it?'

Constantine paused. After a moment he answered, 'Yes.'

'I have not heard of more,' continued Carwithen; 'but that's not saying there were no more. Us don't get news fast here. I knowed a case of a vessel laden with copper, went to pieces in Tonacombe Cove, and the Morwenstowe farmers were still as mice about it till they'd brought up all the ore on donkeys' backs. The neighbours in Kilkhampton and Bude knew nothing about it till the bones were picked clean. That's our ways, hereabouts. We don't talk when we're eating.'

'How many acres are there in Stanbury?'

'About nine hundred, and some of the land first-rate. Come in, sir, and have a drop of comfort. You drank water enough when picked up, I reckon, not to want any of that. Come in, sir, and sit down.'

'Have you heard of another situation, Richard?' asked Constantine.

'No,' answered Carwithen, roughly. 'Stone deaf on that side. I'm very comfortable here, and don't want to go. What is the sense, I ask you, of Squire Featherstone taking on, if I do lend a hand to the runners? I ain't against Scripture. Show me the passage that condemns smuggling, and opens the kingdom of Heaven to gaugers, and I submit. What is there wrong in smuggling? Nobody can say. It's the custom of the country. Wasn't Levi an exciseman, and called away, because it was not a fit occupation for an apostle? Do you mean to tell me that the sons of Zebedee owned a boat and went all about the sea and brought across nothing but fishes? It is not in human nature. It is not credible. I should have no respect for them if they were such fools. Come in, sir. I'll tell you the truth of the matter. Master is a very good man, and great in Scripture. So am I, and because he can't bring down a great text on my head and floor me touching smuggling, he's so put out, he wants to be rid of me. That is the sense of the matter.' He stopped in the door, and turned again to address Gaverock. 'Now, look you here, Mr. Rock. Them two is a pair of innocents. Stanbury, and with it as sweet a turtle-dove as ever were hatched, are to be had for the asking, and the man who gets Stanbury will know better than show Richard Carwithen the door, and object to a keg of brandy, real cognac, left now and again at his doorstep.'

After that visit to Stanbury, Constantine rode back in a meditative mood. 'What a fool I have made of myself!' was the burden of his reflections.

On reaching Marsland he was met by Paul Featherstone.

'Rock,' said the Squire, 'my sister and I have been considering during your absence. We want to ask of you a favour. I am not able to attend to Stanbury as I ought. Would it be possible for me to persuade you to spend the winter with us, and to look after the farm for me?—that is, for Juliot—Stanbury is hers. I need hardly say——' He hesitated, and patted the horse's neck, and looked at the mane. 'We will not ask you to give us your services gratuitously. We will try to make it up to you—but it would be doing me a real kindness, and Juliot a great service.'

'I shall be most happy,' answered Constantine ; 'I have no ties—anywhere.'

CHAPTER XX.

A TEMPTATION.

CONSTANTINE GAVEROCK settled himself to his satisfaction into the situation offered him. He knew from the nature of the man with whom he had to deal that he would be treated with honour and liberality, though no terms were agreed on between them. Paul, indeed, with delicacy, shrank from the mention of money. He knew that Constantine was a gentleman, and with a gentleman money transactions are necessarily awkward to conduct, to spare the feelings on both sides. Constantine was far less sensitive on this point than he was credited with being by Paul Featherstone, and he would rather have been told the amount of his salary than be left to conjecture what it might be.

Constantine had that easy-going temperament which made him adapt himself readily to the place where he was. There were few positions into which he could not accommodate himself, except such as exacted energy and resolution. He liked to waste his day in rambling about the Marsland Farm with Featherstone, riding over to Stanbury to smoke a pipe and drink grog with Carwithen, play on the spinet, and sing with Juliot, and read aloud, or join a game of cribbage in the evening. Scott's novels were then appearing. 'Waverley' had attracted attention; it was quickly followed by 'Guy Mannering' and the 'Antiquary.' Paul Featherstone was not narrow in his reading; he preferred a religious book, as he preferred sacred music, because both appealed to the deep feelings of his soul; but light literature and opera music were not condemned by him. 'Waverley' was procured, and read aloud by Constantine, and both Paul and his sister were so delighted with it that 'Guy Mannering' was purchased for evening reading in like manner.

The days grew shorter and the evenings longer. Very easy days for Constantine, very pleasant evenings for all. Young Gaverock thought of the office of Mr. Nankivel at Exeter, the tedious work of engrossing he had done there, seated on a high stool in a dreary office

with the window looking into a back yard to
the north against a bit of the old crumbling
red sandstone city wall. How monotonous that
life had been! How much better off he was
at Marsland! At Exeter he was under a master.
At Marsland he was his own master.

He looked about him at Stanbury, riding
thither on Paul's cob. He was fond of horse
exercise. At Exeter he had not a chance of
getting astride of a horse. In the office his
hours were from nine to twelve, and from one
to five. Here he regulated his work—such as
it was—according to his own convenience.

Constantine was not an exacting man. He
was not restless by nature, craving for change,
wanting excitement. He was happy to be left
alone, to spend his days in a sleepy, slow manner, and amuse himself with small matters.

He liked a talk with Carwithen, and so
persuaded Featherstone, who was ready to be
persuaded, that the old man was prepared to
abandon his intercourse with the smugglers.

Carwithen never lost an opportunity of
urging Constantine to secure for himself the estate over which he was now but a paid overseer.

Gaverock shook his head and made no answer.

'I shouldn't like to be turned out of this nest, I confess,' mused he; 'so comfortably lined with down, so little to do in it but turn about from side to side and open my mouth to receive my worms.'

One day—it was a Sunday—Constantine was walking with Paul Featherstone from the church. They came to a well, rudely built up, slabbed over with great granite stones, with a gable of solid stepped masonry built up on the horizontal covering slabs.

'By the way, Mr. Rock,' said Featherstone, 'it occurs to me that we have not been told your Christian name. I ask in no spirit of inquisitiveness, but in one of friendliness. Here, when we know and esteem a man, we cease to call him by his surname alone, we call him by both his names.'

'My name,' answered Constantine, 'is John.' He spoke the truth, he was baptized John Constantine. But he did not speak the whole truth.

'Then,' said Featherstone, 'you will suffer us to call you John Rock.'

They were standing by the Holy Well.

'This,' said Constantine, looking down into the water to conceal his face, and speaking so as to change the subject—'this, I presume, is the well of which you spoke to me, as resembling the heart of your sister.'

As he spoke he put his walking-stick into the pool to measure its depth, and he played with it, stirring up the sediment. Paul caught his hand.

'For God's sake,' said Featherstone, hastily, 'do not that. The saying here is, "Who troubles the spring, troubles his soul."'

'The turbidness will soon settle,' said Constantine.

'In the well—yes. In you?—you know best. I tell you only what the people here say. That which is by nature placid soon casts down what clouds it—that which is not as clear takes long to disperse its cloud.'

They walked on, talking. Paul Featherstone was restrained in his manner. Something was on his mind which he desired to say and yet dreaded to utter.

As they neared Marsland he became agitated. He stood still, and laid his hand on the arm of Constantine.

'I wish to communicate something to you,' he said; ' but I must ask beforehand that you will do me justice to believe I speak with the best intentions.' He paused, and Constantine bowed. His heart failed him. Was Paul about to rebuke him, and bid him depart; to tell him he needed his services no longer?

' Mr. John Rock,' said Paul Featherstone, ' we have enjoyed your society during the few months you have been with us, and we are in dread of losing you. I think that I can assure myself that you have been happy at Marsland.' Constantine bowed again. 'I cannot be deceived in what I have seen,' he continued. ' I believe that my sister likes your presence here, as much—even more than myself. We unite in desiring that you will remain. I wish above all things to secure my dear sister's happiness. If—as I almost hope—you are not indifferent to her—and I am sure she is not indifferent to you—why should you not remain here permanently? Excuse me speaking : I thought some modest shrinking on your part might restrain your tongue. For that reason I speak. If I am mistaken, it matters not. Juliot has no idea that I have divined her feelings and am revealing them to you. She shall never know. But if this regard be reciprocal—if——'

Constantine clasped his hand and pressed it, almost wrung it. His emotions, conflicting, tumultuous, would not allow him to speak.

'Your hand tells me I am right,' said Paul.

Constantine did not say No. The temptation came to him—from the best of men, and he yielded. The purest of wells was to be troubled by his base hand.

CHAPTER XXI.

SPRINGTIME.

A YEAR and a half had elapsed—to be exact, nineteen months—since the snowy Goose Fair. Spring had come and was passing into summer. The trees had put forth their green leaves, tender and fresh, and the rushing salty blast from the sea had shrivelled them up and turned them black. Only those protected by shelter had survived. In the dingles, the coombes, under the hedges, the glistening pennywort leaves had spread, the white saxifage spikes of flowers had shot up, the primroses had opened, laughed and faded, and now the stately fox-glove was everywhere tossing its pink bells.

The garden of Towan was not a snuggery in which the flowers could flourish, but the glen of Nantsillan was overrun with them ; plants that had languished at Towan, and had been cast forth, had found their way to the sheltered glen, and run wild there—blue navelwort, pink fumitory, and yellow horn poppy. About Towan the gulls screamed, and the magpies chattered, and the peewits piped, but down in the sheltered glen of Nantsillan thrushes and blackbirds sang and finches cheeped and chirruped.

The sea had thrown aside its winter grey trimmed with white and put on azure and spangles, and the winds exchanged their wail for a plaintive song.

Joyous with summer triumph that coast could never be, with its tortured trees and scanty vegetation, that fought the winds, a guerilla warfare of ambushes. But it could be pleasant, always with an under-note of melancholy in its gaiety.

A change has taken place in Towan since we were last there. Mrs. Gaverock is better, but will never recover her former vigour. When old people descend the scale, they go down, not by steps but by stages. The loss of Constantine had broken her. She was so far recovered that she could attend to some of the little matters that needed attention in the house, but she was delicate and weak, and obliged to rest in her own room much during the day. Dennis Penhalligan came to see her every week and administer medicines to enable her to regain something of her lost strength.

Old Squire Gaverock had not suffered from his exposure in the storm. If it had done anything to him it had toughened and roughened him. Tough and rough he had been before ; he was now, perhaps, even more domineering, exacting, and boisterous than previously. He had a new ambition, now that Constantine was lost, and this ambition made him proud and headstrong and resolute to accomplish it. Gerans had married Rose, and they were now away on their honeymoon. The old man was elate. Rose's money would come to the family head, and the estate of Towan might be considerably extended.

'We'll build up the paddock wall again, and have some deer in it once more. We will, by Golly ! ' he said.

He had despatched Gerans to Truro, on his honeymoon, to look about the house property there of Rose, and see whether it could be disposed of to advantage. There was a tin mine in Kenwyn on her land, bringing in royalties.

Gerans was to inquire into the condition of this
mine, and take advice with the Truro solicitor
whether to sell the land or keep it for a few
years.   Old Gaverock had no idea of business.
He kept no accounts.   When he had money
in his pocket he spent it; he did not waste it
—throw it away—but he spent it, and when
he had no money he lived without.   He could
kill his own sheep and bullocks when he
wanted meat ; he had his own dairy.   He grew
his own corn.   He could live on the produce
of his farm till next court day and the rents
came in again to flush his limp purse.   He was
now somewhat troubled with his responsibility
for Rose.   He received her rents, and muddled
her money with his own.   Sometimes he had
not change in his drawer, where he kept his
cash, then he borrowed the change from the
drawer where he kept Rose's money, and then
forgot what he had borrowed, and put back
sometimes more, sometimes less.   His intention
was to be honest in his dealing with the trust,
but he was by education unfitted to undertake
one.   He had reckoned on the help of Constantine, who, having been given a business
training, would be able to disentangle the

affairs; but Constantine was dead, and the
tangle became more confused. Gerans was of
no use to him. Gerans was reared in the same
want of system as himself. The old man became uneasy in his conscience. He did not
wish to do wrong, and he did not know how
he stood with regard to the trust. So he asked
the help of Penhalligan.

Dennis had a clear head, and was business-
like. He came up continually to Towan to
see Mrs. Gaverock—which was nonsense—old
women can no more be patched up than old
cracked crockery; but he might be of service
in looking into the trust, in arranging the
figures, and in advising about the sale. Gaverock had the idea that lawyers were all rogues,
and that if he consulted a lawyer he would be
given rascally advice. 'One lawyer shovels
into the pocket of the other,' he said, 'as one
hand washes the other hand. But Penhalligan
is a doctor, not a lawyer, so he may be able to
give an unbiassed opinion.' As he regarded all
lawyers to be rogues, he considered all doctors
to be humbugs, as far as their profession affected
them—that is, he considered law to be rascality
and medicine quackery; but a lawyer or a

doctor, taken independently of his profession, might be an honest man. If he were himself unwell, he would not think of calling in a surgeon ; he would ask the opinion of a non-professional, because more likely from the latter to get an unprejudiced opinion. A doctor would protract his illness to extract a larger fee. By degrees old Gaverock came to regard Dennis with respect. He found that he was quite able to see his way through legal documents, and to sift and sort debit from credit entries.

'What is the sense of writing "Debtor" there ? ' said Gaverock, pointing to the head of an account-book. 'I pay my way. It is in-sulting. You'll be putting me down as bank-rupt next. Besides, you are setting down there things I have paid. You may scribble them there if you please, but you won't force me to pay them again.'

With his mind alive to his own incapacity, and with a keen suspicion that the solicitors at Truro were not to be trusted, he was ready to accept advice from Dennis and submit to his opinion in a way he had done to no one else. Dennis Penhalligan had a peremptory, decided manner, and this exactly suited Gaverock. The old Squire readily submitted to be guided through a quagmire in which at every step he took he sank, when he felt that the hand extended to him was that of a man who knew where he was treading. Although he grumbled at Doctor Sawbones giving himself airs, yet he secretly approved of the tone he assumed, and blindly submitted to his advice. Gerans was surprised and Rose annoyed at the influence gained over old Gaverock by the young doctor. The former was unsuspicious of the attachment of Dennis for Miss Trewhella, and the latter was too prudent to waken his jealousy by adverting to it. Rose was annoyed at the influence gained over Mr. Gaverock, because she considered, not without reason, that Dennis was taking a place in the counsels of the family that properly belonged to Gerans, that he was advising and directing concerning her property instead of the man who was shortly to be her husband. Involuntarily, she contrasted Gerans's ignorance with the knowledge of Dennis, the promptitude and intelligence of the latter with the procrastination and stupidity of the former. Gerans was good-natured and easy-going; it never occurred to him to oppose his father; if he formed a contrary opinion, he allowed the old man to overide him, and trample it down, scornfully, whereas if Dennis Penhalligan expressed an opinion the Squire submitted at once.

'Gerans,' said she, one day, pouting and peevish, 'why do you allow Mr. Penhalligan to supplant you as your father's adviser? He is listened to, and no ear is turned to you. He directs and is obeyed; you express a wish and are ignored.'

'My dear Rose, I know nothing about business. Dennis is a very good fellow, has plenty of brains, and is invaluable. If I were to meddle I should muddle.'

'But your father ought to pay attention to your wishes, and not listen to Dennis Penhalligan.'

'What! attend to my advice when I am as ignorant of these matters as a babe!'

'Yes, whether for right or wrong, for good or evil, your opinion should be deferred to.'

'I don't see that, Rose,' said Gerans, good-humouredly.

'I am not at all convinced that Penhalligan's advice is for the best,' urged Rose.

'There we differ. Of course he advises for our welfare. We are friends. He likes you and he likes me.'

Rose's cheek flushed, and a light quivered in her eye. She was tempted to tell him of Dennis's proposal on the night of the Goose Fair, but her better judgment prevailed. She might have done so without exciting jealousy and dislike of his rival in the heart of Gerans. Gerans was so perfectly truthful, right-minded, and good-hearted, that he would have pitied Dennis, not borne him ill-will; he would not have suspected that he continued to harbour a hopeless passion for Rose and to nourish bitter feelings against himself.

For some time before the marriage Rose Trewhella was not in an amiable mood. She was fond of Gerans, but impatient of his placidity and angry at his submissiveness to his father. She saw all his weaknesses, she liked him, but did not love him with all her heart, and she caught herself contrasting him with Dennis, and asking herself which was the better man of the two—better, not as to the qualities of the heart, but of the mind. A little corroding contempt for the easy good-humour of Gerans was seated, like a 'worm i' the bud,' very near her heart. To Dennis she could look up, on him she could lean, he was strong and tall; but at Gerans she must laugh or curl her lip, he was so small and weak where Dennis was great and strong. She was angry with herself for drawing this contrast, because she really liked Gerans and she had no spark of affection for Dennis. Then she thought of Old Michaelmas Day—of her drive with Gerans to Wadebridge, and his proposal; she thought how broad and red he had seemed seated by her in the gig with his greatcoat on and a thick white belcher over his chin, how he had fidgeted over his proposal, and made it clumsily, in a prosaic manner, whilst blowing his nose in a great orange pocket-handkerchief spotted white. She would always associate that most eventful moment of her life with the great yellow bandana kerchief and the white woollen belcher. There had been no passion in his voice; he had been like one labouring to get rid of an irksome duty, great shy booby that he was. Then—on the way home, how different! What fire, what rage, what romance, in the declaration of Dennis! She remembered how she had recovered consciousness in his arms, against his furiously beating heart. She recalled his quivering face, his frantic words, his vehement appeal, his despair. Did Gerans love her? She could not tell. He showed no tokens of passion. Did Dennis love her? Of his love there could be no question. She was irritated at the contrast.

'Gerans,' said she, one day, after she had been thinking about this, 'tell me truly, on your honour, what I desire to know of you.'

'Of course I will, Rose—I keep no secrets from you.'

'Tell me : before you started on Goose Fair day, did your father order you to propose on the road ? '

'*Order!* No, Rose—not exactly that. He *recommended* me to speak to you.'

'That is enough,' she said, and ran to her room, where she burst into tears. She sulked for a week after that avowal. 'He is, indeed, like a well-trained poodle,' she said. 'Never mind, as soon as we are married, I will insist on his taking his own course, and the old man must give way. If he will not, I will not remain at Towan ; I shall make Gerans come with me to Truro, and there we can settle, and be masters in our own house.'

Whilst Gerans and Rose were away on their

honeymoon trip to Truro, Squire Gaverock saw more of Dennis than before. His presence had become a necessity to him. Loveday had not been easy at the frequent visits of her brother to Towan before the marriage. She knew the state of his heart, and she thought that it could conduce to no good that he should meet Rose so often. She saw that every visit made him miserable and gloomy. She heard him pace his room at night and sigh. She noticed how much more worn and thin his face became, and how the lines, hard and bitter, about his mouth deepened. Dennis was becoming irritable towards her as well. He thought she watched him, and he thought right; he did not value the tender love that prompted her to observe him; he regarded her attention as intrusive and inquisitive. He became silent and reserved with her, sometimes he even lost his temper, and spoke roughly to her. Then her eyes filled with tears, and she withdrew, but said nothing, knowing that it was best to leave him alone. She was unaware that he had spoken his heart's secret to Rose; she saw that Rose's engagement was preying on his mind and heart. She tried to hide from him that she saw the trouble he was in, and that she was watchful of him, yet her deep sympathy must express itself, if not by word, at least by act of love; and when he noticed that she saw and pitied his sufferings, he was offended and resented it.

At Christmas he had met with disappointment about his bills. Several were unpaid; payment was delayed, and he was pressed for money to meet certain debts he had contracted for groceries, and drugs, and drapery. He could not pay till he had received his dues, and if he were importunate for his money he might lose his patients. This also helped to fret his temper and make him more despondent in his view of life.

Whilst he was thus troubled, old Gaverock called him in to help him in the management of Rose Trewhella's property. He had loved Rose without any mercenary ideas in his head; but, as he went through the accounts, and examined into her affairs, previous to the marriage, for the drawing up of the settlement, it was forced on him—how he would have been relieved of his embarrassments if only he could have secured the hand of the heiress.

'Take from him the talent, and give it to him that hath ten,' muttered Dennis one day;

'that is the order of the world's government. This world is a school, in which every good thing goes to the favourites, and certain poor boys get only impositions and blows. I have but one luxury left me, one friend dear to my heart, my last, my only consolation. From that I shall be parted.' He set his teeth, and his eyes glared fiercely. 'That will be taken from me, because I am to be utterly badgered, and goaded to madness. My piano—I shall have to sell that, if I can find a purchaser in this desolate land. My piano—my mother's piano! No more Beethoven, no more Mozart and Haydn!' He clenched his nervous fingers behind his back, and his chin sank on his breast. 'Some men are born under a star, and the star may disappear for a while but returns in the sky. I was born under a meteor, whose course is downward, a flare, a few sparks, and then—nothing.'

END OF THE FIRST VOLUME.